where our *stories* leave us

KELSEY LASHER

ISBN-13: 978-1534684683
ISBN-10: 1534684689

Cover Art by Christa Holland of Paper & Sage
Paperandsage.com

Interior Design by Stacey Blake of Champagne Formats
Champagneformats.com

Dedication

To my husband Scott
whose words, actions, and love encouraged me
to make this dream a reality.

I love you with all of my heart!

Prologue

Willa

I read *I Know Why the Caged Bird Sings* in tenth grade. The poem I mean, not the book. I wanted to read the book but honestly, the poem broke my heart into too many pieces to subject myself to the story in there. I know it's shameful of me, to willingly ignore the true story of heartbreak and triumph of another human being, especially one that has triumphed as triumphantly as Maya Angelou but I did all the same because when you're young, you're selfish and you're closed off and everyone seems to be ok with that for some reason. Like everyone knows that soon enough, all teenagers will realize how heartbreaking life is and how little the world cares about them so why not let them be selfish for a while.

True enough I suppose.

I remember the day that Mr. Andrews read it to us. He was one of those teachers who made poetry sound like a monologue. He made anything sound like a monologue really. Even when he read to us from the New York Times

Mr. Andrews read to us with his compelling, heartbreaking voice about the caged bird with its clipped wings and its tied feet and the fearful trill that it uttered. Its singing of the things that it could only dream about but longed for with every fiber of its being and I sat in my chair in the front row with tears running down my face.

Back then when the world was still fresh and new to me, when I was untested and untried and naïve, the beauty of words moved me. The tragedy of a living thing clipped and tied and longing for freedom broke my heart and I could almost hear its feeble song of desperation and pining. Every tweet like a tap of Morse Code spelling out the request for the key.

I pictured that cage and all that it stood for. The oppression and the belittling, the undermining of the humanity within and I hated it. I didn't understand it and felt unbelievable pity for the soul within the cage.

That's what words can do. They can move us and transform us and shape our future. They can inform the trajectory of our lives like signs on a highway.

Even words that aren't beautifully penned by Maya Angelou or written in perfect prose. Words that are spoken can change us too.

Especially when they come from the mouths of paramedics.

After that day, when the men that drove the ambulance, the men with their hands covered in latex and their eyes veiled with sadness and professionalism spoke their words to me, I didn't despise the cage the way I used to. It called to me, pulled me, drew me like a magnet.

I climbed into my car and closed the door and saw in my mind's eye, my wings that were clipped and hemorrhaging, my feet that were tied down in despair and then I looked up and saw my cage. I saw the open door of grief inviting me, pulling me in like a safe haven from a storm.

I saw it and I dragged my heart inside. I slammed the door and decided that I would stay for awhile. A long while because in here, with its bars and its loneliness I could see the outside world full of people that hadn't just been shot down mid-flight like I had. I could watch them and they me, we could talk and I could function, I could still live, but in here, in my cage, I was safe. Nothing could touch me. Nothing could get close enough to destroy me again and I grew fond of it.

I put my heart in its cage and I let it sing all of the sad songs over and over and over again. Songs of the things I had known and longed for still. But I wasn't like the bird in the poem.

I didn't sing of freedom. I never wanted my heart to take flight again.

Chapter 1

Willa

"50 miles to empty".

The car's computer was counting down to the beginning of my future, the tire's treads on the pavement pounding out a drum roll. I didn't know where I was going but my plan had to work. It was too dramatic, too poetic not to.

I glanced down at my radio, wondering if it would be able to pick up any stations yet. I had roamed around in this middle-of-nowhere section of I-25 for far too long and the static in my speakers was starting to get to me. White noise to match a white landscape, flecks of sound swirling into a great cacophony of nothingness like the snow outside my window.

I thought about digging in my center console for my USB cable, thought about plugging in my phone and letting it play on shuffle but that was too risky. I might hear a song that reminded me of before, and that would be a waste of the last 900 miles.

There it was. A voice in the void, cracking and stuttering until it became clear across the FM waves.

"...your Old Town Oldies, where nostalgia is King and memory is Queen."

The opening bars to "September" filled my car, dragging too many memories with them. I punched the dial with my whole hand before I could stop myself, breaking a nail in the process. Tears began rolling down my face and I wiped them away with my ragged and uneven fingertip. The jagged edge of my ring fingernail stood out like a broken fence post. The one that was supposed to have the French tip and princess cut diamond was stubby and unadorned and the bed beneath that the nail should have shielded was bleeding and raw.

Like the heart of a grown woman who had lost her whole world.

That song was too much. Its joy mocked me. Its opening lines haunted me.

I couldn't let myself think about that day, that September day, couldn't let the snow swirl into visions of tulle, a veil over my eyes.

I turned up the speed of the windshield wipers and depended on them to wipe away the flakes, the swirling, the hypnosis that comes from snow and memories pelting my field of vision. I couldn't let my mind wander so I trained it on other things. I tried to count how many swipes per minute the wipers made. It was a challenging task to accomplish while I drove but I risked it. One, two, three, four...

The rhythm became natural and I kept count mindlessly until a minute passed on the clock. 62 swipes. 62 swipes per minute. That was 3, 720 swipes per hour. The wipers had been on for three hours now so that meant that I had seen those blades slide past my vision 11,160 times. I did the math easily in my mind, letting the laws of math, the stability, and sureness of it comfort and soothe me. I could always depend on numbers. They weren't as beautiful or compelling as words or art or music but they were dependable and that mattered. It mattered a lot.

I thought that the song had to be over by now and gathered up my courage. I winced inwardly as I cautiously turned up the radio again. Elvis Presley's silky smooth voice flooded the car like rich, warm whiskey burning as it settled within me.

I didn't want to hear a love song. Especially one about the futility of fighting the feeling of falling in love. I couldn't let myself relate. I couldn't let myself regret the fall I let my heart take and then the way it had shattered at the bottom; The place that love should have been to cushion and cradle and treasure it. He would have if he could have…

I turned off the radio again and let my mind wander. For the eighty-seventh time, I wondered why I had set out on this trip now. A road trip to Colorado in January? It was a fool's errand.

"40 miles to empty." The odometer was as steady as a heartbeat, ticking down the miles to the end of my old life.

I wondered if this would work out like a movie or a perfectly timed novel. I had envisioned that it would when I made the plan but now, I wasn't so sure. I had given myself a limit; fill up the tank three times and wherever I was when that last tank was gone was where I was stopping.

That's where I would live my new kind of living. Starting over and getting my money's worth out of life because now I had his life's worth of money.

I was his beneficiary. Not his wife, I would never be his wife. The life insurance check was written out to me with my maiden name dragging along the long, straight line of the check like a ball and chain behind a prisoner.

Like a U-Haul trailer dragging behind a car that had no idea where it was going.

The snow began to pick up and the radio crackled.

"20 miles to empty," the gas meter said.

The static of the radio cut in and out, making the Beatles voices sound like a disco ball if light could be sound. Flashing in and out of light and darkness, sound and silence, chaos and peace.

I thought about turning it off but there was something oddly comforting about it. It was as if the weather and the radio and my heart were all singing the same song. Like they were saying, "we're here, but not really".

"We feel, but we don't."

"We sing, but we don't."

"We flurry and rage and swirl and freeze."

"But we don't."

Self-pity poured through my car like heat from the vents and it lulled me into complacency and comfort. I was right to leave it all behind. Never mind that they were all sad too. I had to go.

I looked out and to the right just in time to see a sign announcing the next town. I would be in it, a part of its roads and snow in ten miles. That would leave me five miles to spare on this last tank of gas.

This would have to be it. My new home, the place that I would start over with my new, stilted version of living and I hadn't even really paid any attention to the name. Oh well, that seemed about right. It's not like I was trying to move somewhere perfect, some quaint little town where I could live a quaint little life. There was probably no such thing anyway.

My coming here was supposed to be haphazard, unplanned, like the spot where the deflated balloon falls after it's been let go, let loose from the soft, sweet hands of a child to float away. It didn't matter what the place was called. It's where the gas tank had dropped me so I would be staying and that was that.

Unconsciously, I rolled my shoulders back and shook my hair a bit. My sister Quinn calls it my "pistol pose". She always tells me that when I do that, my shoulders pull back like a gun being cocked and at any moment, something: determination, anger, resolve, *something* will shoot out of me like a bullet.

"It's all in your shoulders Wills. It's just right there." She would say trying to push them down jokingly with her hands. "I know the fight is coming as soon as those shoulders pull back and, I'll just go ahead and say right now before it even starts, I surrender!" She would smile at me with her hands in the air and disarm me with it, and slowly my shoulders would slump back into relaxation, the kind that comes from being with your sister.

Quinn. She was devastated that I left, not so much for her sake but for mine.

"How can you choose to just be alone right now Willa? Why would you isolate yourself? That's not going to do the trick. It just won't."

"I know it doesn't make sense to you Quinn but I have to. I just, I can't be *here* anymore. Not with all of the memories. There's too many of them. So many that I can't move. I can't think. I can't..."

She had cut me off with one of her hugs. She could do that; hug. She was one of those women who had mastered the art of touch in a way that made it the answer to everything, to everyone's problems even if you were a perfect stranger. Especially if you were her sister.

"I just have to, ok?" I said into her curly brown hair.

"Well if you have to then you have to. There's no fighting that Iron Wills," she said with a wink. That was the other thing she could do. Quinn could make puns for days and somehow, coming from her, especially in the middle of a hug, they were never annoying.

So there I was, "Iron Wills with her Pistol Pose" ready to meet this new town of mine. The place where no one would force me to acknowledge the past, the heartache. Where no one knew me so no one would know that I wasn't living with my whole heart. Where I could be the new version of myself, the one that considered coping a triumph.

The car pulled its way up a climb in the highway. The elevation was increasing slightly and I could feel it in my faster than normal breathing. This Colorado air was thin and cold and felt just right.

I followed the curve of the highway until suddenly, it opened up into a straight shot and began to descend a little bit. Pine trees and rock formations surrounded me with a picture perfect view of the mountains just ahead and to the right. Snowflakes fell softly in thick, puffy forms, like shaved coconut raining down on me and it covered the rooftops of buildings and houses of all different sizes scattered in front of me. It was like a Dickens Village but a kind of 21st Century version of one.

The air was already thin but what I had left was taken right from me. So much for a non-quaint, non-picturesque, non-perfect place to bury my sorrows and wallow in self-pity.

There was another green sign just to the right, a road marker not just for the road but really, for my life.

"Castleton Next Three Exits" it read.

This place was just plain gorgeous and, even in the fuzzy, hurting place I was in, the one that had filled me with pessimism and darkness, I didn't hate it.

Chapter 2

Willa

I took the second exit for two reasons. The first of which was that I didn't think my car, which was running on fumes at this point, would make it to the third exit. The second reason was that the road was named "Kerfufree Street", a name that just seemed too intriguing to ignore.

If I had driven this road any time before now, when I was my old self and not the sad girl driving to who knew where I would have laughed at it. Out and out laughed, maybe even got out of the car to take a picture next to the sign so that I could send it to Quinn. Today I just kept on driving, though with a mix of relief that I could still recognize some element of humor in everyday life and frustration at that realization as well.

I drove down Kerfufree Street as it looped over the highway and veered to the right landing me smack dab in what looked like the middle of town. Street lights lined the road, ready to glow and shine through the snow and every few yards, giant square planters with pine and poinsettias spilling out stood.

There was a courthouse to my right that looked like it had been built in the 1920's with little houses scattered around it. They looked like sprinkles thrown atop a white, frosted cupcake.

All of them were charming beyond a doubt. I looked away from the quaint cottages to see a few shops up ahead. One called "Pretti in Pink" with sparkly pink curtains and a display of hats in every shape and shade of pink jumped out at me. It stood next to another store who's sign simply read "Feed n' Stuff". Those two buildings lining that small section of Kerfufree Street somehow endeared themselves to me, grabbing onto what little romance was left in my heart. They reminded me of a married couple, one feminine and beautiful the other masculine and hard standing tall and proud and so together in their permanence, clinging to their shared foundation.

I turned my eyes away and kept driving.

There were a few coffee shops here and there, a toy store, a school. My gas light started blinking at this point and I decided to look for a gas station.

I spotted one a block or two ahead of me and kept the car moving in that direction. I figured I had better fill up before I decided what to do next. I hadn't let myself wonder where I would stay or what I would do once I arrived somewhere. I hadn't really wanted to because, even though I had willingly made this trip, willingly made the effort to start over, it would mean that I was starting over and living a life without him.

I pulled into the station and began to pump the gas.

"Ok, Willa, this is it," I told myself. "You have to think about what's next."

I tried to pull my shoulders back in a conscientious effort to meet the future head on. I tried to make myself think and plan, tried to force myself to get out my phone and look for the nearest hotel but I just couldn't.

I closed my eyes to focus but all that popped into my view was his face. It was like it was tattooed onto my eyelids. I quickly opened them, mentally scolding myself for doing that. I should have known better.

The gas nozzle clicked, signaling that it was done, that nothing was stopping me from moving forward but I knew better.

"Quiet you!" I said with a scowl looking down at the nozzle.

I got back in the car, sat behind the wheel and decided that I was simply frozen there. That I couldn't go back to my old life but I couldn't start a new one either. All of it was just too hard and too real and too final and I just couldn't. So, a gas station it would be.

I would be the gas station girl, sleep in my car, live on hostess snacks and Icee's and really bad coffee. I didn't love the smell but that was ok. It might grow on me and maybe it would just be my thing, like instead of Chanel No. 5, I would just smell like gas.

I shook my head and decided that that wasn't the best plan. Even the saddest of the sad don't want to smell like gas.

So, with that option gone, I had to find another but as I sat there, ready to pull out my phone, ready to move *forward*, my hand began to shake and tears filled my eyes because I realized for the millionth time in the last year and a half that this was real and plans had to be made and I had to move forward by myself.

I had stalled out again.

I couldn't face it. Not yet. So I decided that I would just drive around Kerfufree Street some more because wandering around alone seemed less sad and less permanent than settling down alone.

Just as I was about to pull out of the parking lot I saw a restaurant across the street. It was a café really. A café with an inn attached to it.

It was a tall, Victorian building with a turret and all, but, the similarities to the tight-laced, bygone era ended there. The building was painted in a blue as soft as a spring sky with white trim all around. It was nice and peaceful but jarring at the same time because the turret, the cylindrical, protruding turret that some architect had slapped on the left side of the house as a crowning jewel decades ago had been painted to look exactly like a spaceship.

There it was two stories up like a silver bullet that had been shot out of a starting gun and then suspended in flight. The metallic paint surrounded the entire turret save for the window. That was still a window with glass and all but the rest, well the rest of the crazy thing looked like a spaceship. There were even flames painted below, fanning out in jagged tongues of yellow, orange and red down the corner of the house.

I had to go there.

I pulled into the parking lot and realized that it was all painting a picture. The house was the sky and the trim wasn't just straight hard lines of white. The paint had been fanned out and given soft, fluffy edges. It looked like clouds against the pale blue and the space ship looked like it was shooting through the sky, taking off and ready to explore.

A hand-lettered sign with writing prettier than the stars hung down over the front door.

"The Aurora Boreal Inn and Café"

He would have loved this place. He would have photographed it from every angle talking about how it would prove the power of charm better than anything else. How it was art and joy all at once and that had to be put into a frame on a gallery wall. He would have walked inside and put an offer down on it in no time flat and he would have gotten it too. Even if it wasn't for sale because he always got what he wanted. Not because he bullied or pushed or charmed in a slimy, used car salesman kind of way. Because he disarmed you with kindness and a smile and some intangible thing that made you want to make him happy forever and always because he made you happy no matter who you were.

He would have loved it and somehow, that made this place the perfect square one.

I parked my car in the small parking lot, got out, and pulled my coat around me. The snow had slowed and the sun was beginning to peak out like a nosy neighbor peeping behind her blinds but it was still freezing out. I took the two steps up onto the front porch and opened the door. There were tiny little bells that jingled as I walked in, signaling my arrival and I looked up just in time to meet the smiling gaze of a woman behind the counter. The rest of the place was empty, probably because it was 2:30 in the afternoon and no one really eats at that time of day.

The woman had hair as fiery and unruly as the flames painted down the side of the cafe that would have probably flown right into her face had it not been for the headband she was wearing but something about it was beautiful. Maybe it was its effortless, effervescent, freedom that just made you want to grab ahold of it and go for a ride. Or maybe I was just jealous that my brown, stick straight hair wasn't that full and fun but either way, I liked it.

"Well hey there," she said. "Come on in and warm up! Can I get you started with some coffee or tea? Why don't you just sit down right here while you decide!" She had come around to the front of the counter and was swinging a stool out for me like there was someone in it who had just had their hair cut and was about to look in the mirror for the first time.

I didn't necessarily want to. Didn't want to sit down and be forced to chit chat with this woman but what could I do?

"Uh, thanks," I said. "Coffee sounds nice."

"Comin' right up! I think you'll like it! I brew it with just a touch of cinnamon and vanilla in the grounds, and, well, I got to say, it's like Christmas and Heaven and all things comforting in one little cup!"

She was finished pouring before I even got my coat off.

"Cream and sugar?" She asked.

"I think I'll take it black today," I said.

"Well, that settles it then."

"Settles what?"

"Well, when you walked in here, I thought you had a tough look about you. Not in a bad kind of way just kind of determined and, well, strong you know? I've owned this place for twelve years now and I have a theory that only strong people take their coffee black. I've seen it time and time again. I should really document my findings, publish some kind of scientific study on it but probably no one would read it. That's how I take mine too," she said with a wink.

I wanted to roll my eyes at her because how could you tell something like that about a person just by the way they drink their coffee. I didn't though. I thought I better not let rudeness be the other adjective she attributed to me. I'd let something else silly like how much ketchup I used or whether I ordered a house versus a Caesar salad tell her that. Besides, she was way off. I wasn't strong in the least.

"Oh, I don't know about that," I said with a little chuckle.

"My theory is never off sweetie. Never. Maybe you don't think you're strong but you wouldn't be turning down cream and sugar if you weren't. Only a strong stomach can handle black coffee and I say a strong stomach goes hand in hand with a strong heart."

"Well, if you like black coffee so much, why the cinnamon and vanilla?" I asked with a little more edge to my voice than I meant to have. I felt bad but I was a tad bit annoyed by her assessment of me. I wasn't ready for someone to tell me I was strong. I wasn't ready to stop being weak. To stop wallowing.

"Oh, that? Well, that's because even the strongest people need some flavor in the blackest, darkest, cup they've been given."

She held my gaze then as she leaned on one elbow on the counter. She might as well have been looking right into my heart. I didn't know what to say so instead, I just picked up the powder blue mug that said, "Shoot for the stars" in white cursive print and took a sip of coffee.

And that coffee was everything she promised it would be. Comfort and flavor right in the middle of my darkness.

"Ah, there you see? Delicious isn't it? Just what you needed?"

I swallowed, cleared my throat and said "Yes, thank you," Just before I looked away from her mysteriously knowing gaze.

"Your café is charming." I was trying to change the subject but it really was delightful.

There were booths lining both sides of the room. Each one had a stainless steel table in the middle and tufted, off-white seats on either side. They looked more like couches than booth seats and I wanted to curl up in each one. The middle of the room had small tables with the same stainless steel tops but with cream, filigreed legs curling out underneath and cozied up to everyone were simple, sky blue chairs.

The walls were divided by a chair rail painted the same white as the trim outside and it looked like a shooting star flying around the room. The bottom half of the walls were painted a navy blue and the top was a soft gray. Then there was the ceiling, the tall, sweeping ceiling. It was painted the same dark blue but with stars painted freehand all over. There were the Little Dipper and Orion's Belt and another constellation that looked like a little boy in a spaceship waving down below.

On every table, there were little, white vases in the shape of spaceships with fresh yellow daisies shooting out like golden jet fuel.

On the far side of the room, opposite the counter was a small stage. It was framed by navy blue curtains and had Christmas lights strung over it like a roof over a carriage. The wall behind it read "The Stars Are Shining."

"It's what I think a spaceship would look like if a woman got to decorate it," I said.

The woman laughed at that and said "Well thank you very much! I suppose that's what I was going for!"

"So, why the space theme? Did you want to be an astronaut growing up or something?" I said. There was no one else in this place, no hope for any distractions from this woman digging right into me and why it was that I needed that cup of coffee so I needed to do all that I could to keep her off track.

"Oh no, the space theme isn't for me. No, when I opened this place up 12 years ago, my son was five and completely, 100% obsessed with all things Outer Space. Things hadn't been completely great for our family up until then and well, this was our fresh start. I wanted him to feel that too, wanted to make his dreams come true as well as mine so, when I saw this place on the market with the turret and everything, well, I knew that I had to go for it. I knew it would be our perfect blast off!" She said. She clapped her hands together and shot one up in the air as she said "blast off" and, Lord help me, I was beginning to like this woman.

"How fun!" I said. "I'm sure he loved that! What's his name?"

"Drew. My Drew," she said and as the name left her lips, I swear that everything about her, her green eyes and dancing hands and crazy hair, all of it, softened and melted like ice cream in the sun.

"How about you, what did you want to be when you grew up?" She asked me.

"Me? Umm well, all kinds of things really. In third grade, I was sure I was going to be an ice dancer."

I paused then and my mind raced back in time to Ollie and me, skating across the ice rink at the YMCA. I was no good, clumsy and unsteady but he held me up while he sang the theme song to

"Sesame Street" at the top of his lungs.

He sang every line of that song from start to finish while I laughed so hard I nearly fell. He held out the last line for way too many beats, emphasizing it with a full vibrato and a sweep of his hand and then we fell to the ground in fits of laughter while the rest of the crowd looked at us with scrunched up noses and snickers behind their hands.

"There," he said. "There was music, there was a crowd, and you were moving on skates. You can now say that you are an ice dancer! Let's just say that you had to go into early retirement due to, hmm… laughingitis!"

I forced my mind to return to the present but not before I thought, "What I wouldn't give to suffer from that now."

"An ice dancer would be fun! So are you an ice skater then?" The woman that was standing in front of me, the real person here with me, not the one I was missing with every hope and dream and feeling in my body, asked me.

"Not even close," I said trying to push away the memories. "No, I'm just an accountant."

"An Accountant you say? Aren't you just a breath of fresh air!"

"I have to say, no one has ever said *that* about my profession before!" I said, laughing a little. How did this woman push me to tears and laughter in a matter of seconds like this? She was like a roller coaster personified in the best way possible.

"Well, it's just that I've been looking for an accountant to help me with the business side of things here. I'm pretty skilled in the decorating and cooking and hosting and all that jazz but the numbers? Oh, the numbers are my Kryptonite! I think you would be perfect at it, though!"

I laughed again at that. "You don't even know me! How do you know I'm any good?"

"Remember? The black coffee? I know you." She said while she pointed her finger at me like she was picking me out of a lineup.

More laughter at this point from me. "You don't even know my name or if I live here or anything about me."

"Alright, alright." She brushed her hair back with her hands and stood up straight in, what I guessed was her "all-business" manner of speaking. "What's your name? Do you live here?"

"My name is Willa Durham and, well, I guess I live here now, kind of. I mean, I just got here and don't really know... I mean the gas tank told me to stop here...it's complicated."

"Well Willa, my name is Lil. It's short for Lillian but I've always thought that the name Lillian should have a 'Dahhhling' after it and I'm just not a 'Dahhling' kind of pehhhson if you know what I mean. So, I go by Lil," she said in an imitation of a stuffy British accent. "So, will you be my accountant? You can even stay here at the Inn for free if you need while you work on my books!"

I hesitated for a moment while I thought back on what brought me to this moment in time. I had stopped here because it drew me, drew me to Ollie but here, in this crazy, cozy place, I was given the next step away from him. The answer to my question of what to do and how to start without him. It was just dropped into my lap, poured into my cup like coffee and I couldn't think of a reason why I shouldn't.

"Ok, Lil. I'm all yours."

Chapter 3

Willa

We walked up a straight staircase, the banister painted the same navy blue as the walls with white spindles shooting up and down between like a perpetually bouncing ball leaving smoke trails behind. I had left most of my stuff in the trailer attached to my car but had managed to grab my overnight bag before Lil hauled me up to "The prettiest and funnest rooms I'd ever see."

I had told her that "funnest" wasn't a word to which she replied,

"If we went around only saying things that were official words, we wouldn't capture the fullness of life. Why limit ourselves, Willa? How else are you going to say that something is super fun? I suppose you could say "the most fun" but that just seems too long and cumbersome and it goes against the *spirit* of the word 'fun' in my opinion."

She didn't even get winded when she said it climbing up all

of those stairs either. You would think that climbing one-hundred-year-old steps while starting a diatribe against the rules of the English language and breaking them in the process, all in Colorado altitude would take it out of a person but it seemed to me that Lil could simply do or say anything in a way that other people couldn't.

It was just "funner" for her that way I guess.

"Over there is the spaceship room," she said. "That's Drew's. He'll be home from school any time now and I'll be sure that you get a chance to meet him. Everyone should have a chance to meet my Drew, Willa. He's one that you shouldn't miss!"

I loved the way she talked about her son. There was no hiding her adoration for him. I didn't know him yet but I could sense just by the spirit of the place that those two, Drew and Lil, must belong to each other the like moon belongs to the stars.

I was struck by a pang of jealousy at the beauty of that. Of having a person that was yours, that you could love and adore and let everyone know about it.

"Over there is my room," Lil said pointing to the room right next door to Drew's. "Feel free to come by anytime. I'm a night owl so really, anytime."

We walked past three other rooms until we got to the end of the hall. Lil stopped and began hitting her hands on her thighs, making a drum roll sound until she said, "And without further ado, this is your room!"

I opened the door to find a canopy bed draped with gauzy, white linen. There was a pale blue comforter with fluffy white pillows and a window seat on the opposite side of the wall, full of cushions and sunlight. The room was classy and fine but all throughout, there were tiny touches of what I was starting to think of as "Lil Charm". A sculpture of an alien stood on the dresser behind a sign that said, "I come in peace." In swirling cursive letters. There were towels folded on the edge of the bed that were embroidered with the words "we don't like 'em smelly", and there was a pillow tucked in the back of the bunch on the window seat that looked like the moon as actual cheese.

The wall was painted an eggshell white, mirroring the delicate but full feel of the room, like the peace and quiet and beauty of the place was suspended in mid air like it could fall and crack at any moment because it was just too perfect.

But somehow, I knew that here, at the end of this hall, it simply wouldn't.

"Thank you, Lil, it is absolutely perfect."

"Still not going to say 'funnest' huh?" she asked me with a nudge.

"Maybe some other time," I said with a half smile.

"Well, you just settle in here for a bit but don't get too comfy. We've got a full night tonight if you're interested. Drew will be home soon along with a few of the other guests so you'll definitely have to come and meet them. Then later tonight, we have Sinatra Night!"

"Sinatra Night?" I asked.

"Yeah! I'm sure you saw the stage downstairs? Well, every Tuesday night we have some kind of performance on it. We'll have bands or poets or artists or whatever but it's great! People from all over town come and we just enjoy each other and the talent! Tonight, we're having my brother's band come play and they're going to do all Sinatra hits. And if that's not enough to entice you, then come for the food. You've got to eat right?"

"I'm pretty tired from the drive but I'll think about it. Thanks."

She looked at me again before she turned to go with those piercing eyes and I knew that she saw me, like, really saw me, but I didn't care. She could see whatever she wanted. I wasn't hiding the fact that I didn't have any joy to spare, especially for a room full of small town Sinatra lovers and their cover band.

I closed the door behind Lil and retreated into myself. I looked around the beautiful room with fresh flowers on the nightstand and thought that it would have made a nice romantic retreat.

The kind that Ollie would have tried to surprise me with after our wedding but that I would have figured out before we even left. He always said that I could read him like a book but I always said that it was because he never tried to hide his pages.

My mind began to wander to him and his face and his laugh and the way that he never kept me guessing. I began to fall down that rabbit hole of remembering again, the one that I had driven hundreds of miles to avoid because the fall and the tumbling down and the landing in a crumpled heap at the bottom were just too painful. So, I pulled out my phone and called Quinn.

She picked up after the first ring which is what I expected. She had obviously been waiting with bated breath for this call.

"So you're there?" Quinn asked on the other end of the line. "I mean you're someplace? Like you've stopped driving and you're at whatever spot you're at?" Not even a hello, just jumping right in full of excitement and energy and worry. That was Quinn.

"I am. It's called Castleton. Castleton, Colorado."

"Colorado, huh? Is it pretty?"

"It is! This town is as cute as they come too. Full of charm and based on the woman who owns the Inn I'm staying at, full of characters."

"I like characters! They're my kind of people!"

"You would like it here Quinn, the Inn is in this old Victorian house but the turret on the outside is painted to look just like a spaceship blasting off. The owner painted it that way because her son was obsessed with space when she bought the place and she wanted to make him happy. It's sweet."

"So sweet, Wills! She sounds great! What's the place called?"

I smiled a little to myself before I answered because I knew that my pun-loving sister was going to love the name of the place. "Are you ready? It's the Aurora Boreal Inn."

"Well! This woman is my kind of character! I have to meet her which is my perfect and not so sneaky excuse to come and see you. How are you, Wills?"

"I'm good enough at this moment to not want to talk about how I am."

"Message received. So, what else?"

"I don't know, there's some 'Sinatra Night' thing tonight downstairs in the Café. Lil, that's the owner's name, by the way, really wants me to go. Oh, and did I mention that she also wants me to be her accountant?" I shook my head again at the way that Lil made events turn on a dime.

"That's great, Willa! That'll be just the thing to get you in a new rhythm. The Sinatra night I mean. The accounting is still as boring as ever to me but hey, those numbers sing to you so whatever!"

"You should be grateful for that Quinn! How else would you have passed any of your math classes?"

"Yes, yes, I know! You are my Pythagorean Hero. Seriously, though, you should go to that thing tonight."

"I don't know..."

"What else are you going to do Willa?"

Her voice sounded like she was trying to be nonchalant but I could hear the undertone of worry there.

"I don't know, read a book or something."

"No, you won't, Wills. You'll sit in your room and think about Ollie and then you'll end up in a crying heap and, no one will be there to pick you up. I know it's good to think about him, I think about him all of the time, but sometimes, for a few minutes at least, you've got to let yourself search for life and happiness."

I let silence stretch across the line, let it fill it up because my words were pushed down by tears. I knew she was right but I didn't know how to do that, how to search for life and happiness without him. He *was* my life and happiness.

"Just try Willa," The gentleness in her voice seemed to brush the tears off of my face.

"Ok," I said. "I'll try."

* * *

I could hear the crowd downstairs. A jumble of voices and laughter and dishes clanking together floated up through the floorboards along with the smell of whatever Lil was cooking.

I could smell onions and carrots and beef so I assumed it was pot roast. I love pot roast. My stomach grumbled, adding its demanding voice to the sounds from downstairs. I didn't want to go down, though. Not yet anyway. I wasn't ready to be friendly and make small talk and clap for the small town band. They were warming up downstairs. Random screeches from the sound equipment and chords on the guitar told me so.

My stomach was starting to growl in tune with them.

In an effort to put off the inevitable trip downstairs caused by my apparent starvation, I tried to think of everything else that the food could be instead of Pot Roast. Maybe that would help.

"Maybe it was Beef Stew. Mushy, gloopy, beef stew. With mushy carrots and mushy potatoes and beef that's as tough as jerky. No way did I want that. I would rather eat... Well, I would rather eat Pot Roast." I said out loud to the empty room.

This was not working.

Going down there wouldn't work either, though. I was in no mood to have a nice evening with nice people and nice music. I was grieving, wasn't I? I had come here to grieve. To be just sad enough not to forget him but far enough away that I could be happy enough by not having the life we had thrown around at me like dodge balls in gym class.

No, I couldn't go down there. An empty stomach and a lonely room went along much better with grief than food and fun.

Just then, the band dove into the opening chords of "Fly Me to The Moon."

I could hear an acoustic guitar, a drummer, and what I thought was a stand-up bass. There were no horns. I had never heard Sinatra without horns. It seemed odd, almost sac religious to play Jazz standards with only acoustic instruments. I had always thought that you couldn't have one without the other. I had thought that the songs wouldn't be Jazz, wouldn't stand or play or sing without the horns blaring in their brassy way.

But there it was, as clear as could be from a floor away, the song I'd always known floating up to me in a new form. It was still just as lovely, as plucky, as fun as always.

It was itself, even without the horns.

The drummer kept the beat on the symbols while the guitar strummed adding rhythm and melody all at once. I could hear the bassist walking his fingers up and down the strings, could just picture him sitting there with the instrument in front of him as he swayed it like a lady in arms.

Then there was the vocalist. He jumped in on the downbeat like a kid diving into water. His voice was deep and smooth with a vibrato that made it sound like his vocal chords were dancing.

It was a smile in a song.

I sat there, empty stomach and all and tried to file this away, this knowledge that what I'd always thought was the mark of Jazz could be taken away. That the music could still be itself without that element that's so loud and in charge. It was the horns that took up the bandstand after all, wasn't it? They were the "big band" of the "big band" era, right? But here I was on Sinatra Night at the Aurora Boreal Inn listening to Jazz, *Jazz* without it.

I wondered what Sinatra would think. Would he be disappointed with the way it all turned out? Was he married to the horns? Like, would he show up here tonight with his fedora and smile and charm to beat all charm and just say "Hey fellas, lets just not, alright?"

I decided he couldn't hate what I was hearing too much. The singer of whatever this band was called was doing a great job.

Still, I couldn't help but think about the implications of this whole thing. If you could take something so familiar and expected and change it, what did that mean? Nothing was set in stone.

The guitar went into a solo then, the solo that I had heard done by a trumpet or a flute before was played by someone strumming and picking and drumming on their guitar. His fingers must have been moving so quickly over the strings. I lost count of the number of notes he played. I began to snap my fingers unconsciously and hum the tune to the empty room.

And just like that, this was the song I knew. I would forever have a section of my mind that knew "Fly Me to The Moon" without horns. With a guitar.

I was pulled out of my own wonderings with the sound of knuckles on my door and the voice that followed.

"Umm, excuse me, Miss Durham? I have some food for you. My mom sent me."

I opened the door to find a teenage boy standing in front of me. He had dark brown hair and eyes as blue as the outside of the Inn. I guessed it was actually the other way around, though, that the outside of the Inn was as blue as his eyes. This must be Drew.

"Hi! Oh, my mom is Lil by the way. That probably didn't make much sense before. Why would some random mom send you food?"

"I figured! You're Drew then?"

"Guilty," he said with a shrug that made the dishes on the tray he was carrying rattle a little.

"Well, I'm so glad to meet you, Drew! Your mom would have probably kicked me out if I didn't!"

He blushed a little then but never looked away. "Yeah, my mom doesn't hide how she feels. I kind of like that about her. When I was little, it worked really well for me! I could always tell when she was upset and I was about to be in trouble so I could turn on the charm or grab her a cookie to quell the storm."

I laughed then at the picture of a sweet little boy with puppy dog blue eyes and a gap where his two front teeth should be standing before the wild-haired Lil with a cookie in his outstretched hands.

"I bet you got out of plenty of pickles with that strategy."

"Not as many as you'd think. She caught on pretty quick. Eventually, she would take the cookie, set it on the counter and say, 'We'll have that later after we deal with this.' And we would, we would have a cookie together later." He smiled and his eyes filled with the same melty look that Lil got when she talked about him.

These two.

"Anyway," he said. "My mom noticed you hadn't come down to eat and thought you might be hungry. She sent up a tray but told me not to hand it over without trying to persuade you to come downstairs to eat it. She said I had to give it the 'good ole' college try.'"

"College huh?" I said eyeing the tray, it was pot roast I had been pining for and it looked delicious.

"Yes! And I know what you're thinking! You're thinking that I haven't even been to college yet right? So how could I give it the 'ole' college try?' Well, you just have to think about it this way. If you don't come down the stairs, not only will I be so discouraged with my abilities to give things a collegiate effort with any hope of success, but my mom will be so disappointed in me that she won't even pay for the whole thing." He looked at me then with a smile and a twinkle in his eyes.

This boy was not one to miss just as Lil had said and I couldn't let him down.

"Alright, Drew. Fine. You've persuaded me! I'll come down and eat but only because I want you to go to college. This is all for your education ok?" I said with a wink.

"Got it!"

* * *

The pot roast was better than it had smelled and I decided that if Lil hadn't offered to let me stay at the Inn, I would have accepted payment for my accounting services in just pot roast and coffee. I would maybe even be tempted to work at half speed just so I could have more of the stuff. It was probably better that that wasn't our arrangement in the end.

I cleaned my plate and enjoyed every bit.

By the time I arrived, everyone had been served so Lil and Drew took a seat at a table with me.

"Well, what do you think Willa? Was it worth abandoning your room for?"

"The pot roast is perfection, Lil! I could eat this all day long!"

"Of course, it is, sweetie! I don't need you to tell me that. No, I was talking about the music!" She gestured to the band that was playing "Come Fly with Me".

I had been right with my guesses about the instrumentation but where I thought there were four people, there were only three. The singer and guitarist were one and the same. Two instruments embodied in one person and what a person he was.

He had a master and ease of the music like I had never seen. He knew how to massage it with subtlety until, all of the sudden, he threw in a grand solo. I decided that if the pot roast I was eating could be music, it would be this man's music; comforting, delicious, and soul filling all at once.

"The band is as good as the pot roast Lil."

"Well, I don't know about all that," she said with a smile and a wink. "They are pretty good, though."

"You said one was your brother?" I asked between bites of potatoes soaked in gravy.

"He's the lead guy, the singer/guitarist. That's my Uncle Jake." Drew jumped in.

Once he had been claimed, I started to look at the man to find the family resemblance. His hair was similar to the color of Drew's but he had Lil's striking green eyes. The lower half of his face was covered in a well-trimmed beard but even underneath that, I could see that he and Lil shared the same square jawline. He kept singing while he looked over at our table and smiled at Drew and Lil and it was as if his teeth were soldiers all lined up straight and strong to greet us.

"You'll have to tell him that they're doing a great job for me."

"You can tell him yourself after the show, Willa!" Lil said.

This woman was stretching me like a rubber band.

"Oh, umm yeah sure."

I had no intention of doing that but somehow Lil had a way of working past my intentions and getting me to do things that I didn't want and then making me secretly enjoy it. Still, I planned on finishing my food and heading back upstairs.

That plan went out the window when Lil slid a plate of Apple Pie across the table to me though and with every bite of flaky crust and cinnamon-covered fruit, my resolve melted.

I had a full stomach and was surrounded by new friends, good music and the most welcoming and weird ambiance I had ever experienced. I was becoming a part of the scene, a part of the happiness and peace and pretty little picture. I hadn't realized that I had slipped into a little bit of contentment but I had. The evening was surrounding me like sweatpants after a long day at work, soft and stretchy to fit and comfort all of me.

I was enjoying it. I even laughed when the band began a version of "My Way" and Lil crashed the show, stealing the mic from her brother at the very end and finishing it off with a grand flourish of voice and hand gestures.

I was beginning to think that this was a good idea, this coming downstairs but then they played the song.

It was my sad song, the one that I had played on repeat for days after I lost Ollie. I had sat there in his house, with his flannel t-shirt wrapped around me, with his running shoes still laying in the middle of the front hallway, right where he'd left them, with his half-empty coffee mug sitting on the coffee table and listened to the song until I couldn't cry anymore.

Lil's brother dove into the lyrics of "What'll I Do" with his deep, beautiful voice. It filled the room with feeling and the sounds of the color blue. Most people just swayed and smiled, enjoying the pretty song but each minor chord, each word, ripped me open.

The tears were coming. I could feel their invasion as well as I could feel the pull of the pit. I was falling hard and fast out of the comforting softness of the night into the deep dark hole of sadness. I knew what was coming. I had been on this fall before, the one where your heart thinks it's found solid ground only to have the surface dissolve right out from under you.

Happiness was a trap door. I had stood on it again and now I was falling through. Down, down, down…

"Are you ok Willa?" Lil asked. I could see the concern in her and Drew's eyes but I couldn't find a way to take it from them. It was the same look that Quinn had when she came over to Ollie's every day after work to find me sitting in that same place on the couch, with all that he had left surrounding me like ghosts.

"I just need to go back upstairs."

"Are you sure? Can I get you anything else? At least stay till the song is over."

"No!" I said rather harshly but she didn't understand. It was the song that I had to avoid.

"I'm sorry but, no," I said as I adjusted my tone. "Thank you so much for dinner. I'll see you in the morning."

And with that, I bolted up the stairs, threw open the door and sobbed into my pillow.

Chapter 4

Willa

I'm not artistic. Oh, how I wish I was in some small way but I'm just not.

I tried to be as a kid. I tried everything under the sun; ballet, piano lessons, painting, pottery, if it was offered at the rec center or my school, I was there. Even as a kid, I knew that art held so much beauty and power. Like the ocean or a mountain range. Somehow, it just moved people in a way that nothing else could and for a stubborn and passionate girl that wished the world could think and feel like I did, well, that was a power I wanted.

I kept trying (and failing) at various art forms until the eleventh grade. I sat down with my guidance counselor ready to pick an elective, like a kid looking in on a candy case debating on what brightly colored sweet to pick. I saw the wary look in her eyes before the words came out of her mouth.

"Miss Durham," she said, with her eyes squinted up in some absurd way, like she was blinded by the words she had to say to me.

Like she just couldn't look at them.

"Are you sure you want to take another art class? Why not go for the debate team instead? I'm sure you would be so good at that!"

I paused with my finger on the class list and looked up at her and then at the ugly painting behind her desk. Some sort of beige, wilted flowers lay flat on the canvas. It looked like wadded up tissues falling off of pipe cleaners. The table they were sitting on wasn't half bad but the rest of it was the definition of uninspiring. I knew she had a daughter that was a few years older than me, she had been in Quinn's class actually and everyone thought she was such a gifted artist.

I saw her swirly initials, a loopy "AR" in the bottom, right-hand corner of the tissue painting and briefly thought to myself that those were the only pretty thing on the canvas.

"That was what passed as gifted art in this school?" I thought to myself.

I just couldn't stand for it. Somehow, every less than mediocre piece of artwork that I had ever made fell away from my memory like the petals falling off of the tissues in the painting. If it was the debate team she wanted, that's what she would get. Right here. I pulled back my shoulders and looked at her straight on.

"Mrs. Rodgers," I said in as even and sweet a tone as I could muster. "I know that I'm not as gifted as your daughter Amber," I crossed my fingers behind my back at this point and my toes and my legs and it was all I could do not to cross my eyes too. "But I'd like to try just one more class. I'm sure that will be alright with you since you have such an appreciation for art and, well, you wouldn't want to squash a girl's dreams would you?"

Mrs. Rodgers looked behind her at what might as well have been an advertisement for "Kleenex" hanging on her wall and smiled.

"Well I certainly do appreciate art and I know you do too. I just want to make sure that you understand how important it is that you maintain your 4.0 GPA if you want to stay on track with your goal of attending a top college. I know that art classes haven't been your strength in the past and well…"

My face flushed at this a little. She was right of course but I had to try. I had always been a top student, especially in math and science. It just came easily to me, numbers and facts, and I was ok with that. I was glad, I really was but a part of me longed to engage something more. I had to be more than my brain. I wanted my heart to be discovered too.

"I'll just give it one more chance Mrs. Rodgers. How about something easy like Photography?"

"Alright Willa, photography it is but I'll advise you not to let your efforts there take too much time away from your AP classes. Those will carry you towards your goals." She said with her finely tweezed blonde eyebrows raised.

"I understand Mrs. Rodgers," I said but all I could I think about were the poignant images that I would capture, the Pulitzer Prize I would win someday with the talents that I was about to discover in the dark room of the school.

Those dreams carried me through to second period the next day when I stood before the entrance to my artistic future i.e. the photography classroom. I pictured it as a portal into the unknown, a grand gateway into the world of beauty and all the things that move hearts and awaken minds. This would be it.

Looking back on that day now, I realize that it indeed was all of those things. Not because I learned how to be an artist, though. No, it was because there, in that room, was a masterpiece, *my* masterpiece.

Oliver's hair was like a cup of coffee with too much cream and sugar mixed in. Not quite brown but not quite blonde either. It was thick and rich like coffee too. Like coffee swirling in a cup around a spoon, his hair swirled in perfect curls around his face. And oh, his face. It was the kind of face that could make painters paint and writers write for days and days and days.

His face wasn't so much a face as it was a smile, a smile that took over his blue eyes and his just right nose. It reached up and out and then in. Into you, into your heart and mind and soul.

He sat right in front of me that first day and it was all I could do not to run to the back of the room, grab a camera and take pictures of every strand of his hair, the angle of his shoulders, the way his hand stood up tall in the air when he answered a question in a way that combined confidence and ease like peanut butter and jelly.

And then he turned around and talked to me and I knew then and there that my heart had been discovered.

"You're Willa, right?" he said.

"Yes," I said. I would have said yes to anything he asked me. He could have dared me to go swimming with sharks wearing a swimsuit made of bacon and kelp and "Yes!" would have been my resounding answer.

"Yeah I thought so. I've seen you around I think but I've never really met you. I'm Oliver but my friends call me Ollie. You can too if you want."

And before I even knew what I was saying, before I could see the words that had dropped into my mind like a drunk person sky-diving, before I could reach out and snatch them back because they would just be oh so humiliating, I said this: "You mean *I* can be *your* friend Ollie?"

That perfect boy let out a laugh that sounded like Christmas Morning and my birthday and the fourth of July all rolled into one.

"Well, you called you me Ollie so you must be. You can't ever call me Oliver now though or I'll think this whole thing is over. How do I know that I'm your friend though Willa? What can I call you?"

"My sister calls me Wills," I said with a shrug.

"That's no good. Sounds too boyish and you're anything but boyish." He didn't flush like I did then, just looked straight at me, holding my gaze to make sure I understood that he was telling me that I was beautiful.

"Well then, Ollie, I guess you'll just have to call me Willa and we'll know that every time you say it, you're promising to be in my life and be my friend."

"You've got a deal, Willa," he said as he grabbed my hand to shake it.

He would say the same thing when I agreed to marry him ten years later. He would grab my hand and shake it and say "You've got a deal, Willa." And I would say "I better Ollie."

Then we would laugh and smile and see our faces reflected in my ring. We would celebrate with friends that night at his gallery where he had switched out all of the photographs produced by the most up and coming artists in Austin for pictures of us. Pictures that he had taken of me or pictures that he had taken of both of us, full, life-size, beautiful pictures of us.

I'll never forget the way that they stood guard over us in our happiest moment, surrounding us with our history, our story, the art that was Ollie and Me. I'll never forget the way that my heart felt so full and so heard because well, ever since that day in Photography class he had been my art.

He had filled the need to produce beauty and poignancy and captivating, all-encompassing, life-changing art because that's what we had become. With Ollie, I got to tell a story. With the full and wide and small and succinct strokes of everyday life, we had painted the picture of love and of two people becoming each other's world and sky and stars and air and water and *everything*. Of two people growing together to form the tree in Van Gogh's "The Starry Night."

We were a masterpiece He and I but like a painting or a photograph, we were just a moment in time, captured in print, in two dimensions and nothing I could do could make the picture come to life again.

* * *

They say that the best way to learn a language is to be immersed in it. If you want to learn French, you should move to France, if you want to learn Spanish, you should move to Mexico, and so it goes. They say this is the best way to understand the language, to learn to speak it, to become a part of the culture that communicates with it. I always thought that this must be true, like some kind of conventional wisdom that's right up there with "An apple a day keeps the Doctor away." I didn't really doubt it but I didn't fully relate to it until I spent the morning in the Café with Lil.

The moment I walked down the stairs I was immersed in daytime in a way that I couldn't remember.

Sunlight streamed in through the Eastern facing front windows like water through cracks in a jar. It just leaked and saturated everything in the room, bouncing off of the stainless steel surfaces like light had been sent to dance its way around us. We were flooded by it and it overtook us. Every ray reached its fingers out and over every surface and they wound their way around the room like an army invading.

Like an army of light invading the darkness.

There had to be shadows somewhere, some little corner that was blocked by a chair or a customer that wasn't touched by it but I couldn't see it and as I stood there at the foot of the stairs, I was immersed in the smell of bacon and coffee and blueberry muffins and sunlight.

Immersed in that morning, that day. It had washed over me

and taken over me. I felt its fingers of light pulling at the threads of darkness around me like it wanted to unravel the itchy, bulky fabric that I had wrapped around my heart. There was nowhere to hide from it, from this light and daytime and new fresh start. I had been taken up in its grasp.

In that moment, I forgot the language of sadness that I had been speaking ever since the band had played the song the night before and let myself be swept up in the yellow glow that smelled like warmth and bacon.

I knew that there would be a moment again soon where I would slip back into my native tongue, where I would forget how to feel like this. That was how grief worked. Like your life was the sunshine streaming through the windows one minute and then like a giant cloud had come and wedge its way in front of the glowing ball of fire and happiness the next. Like a big bully that cut you in the roller coaster line as a kid. You're ok with it for a little bit until you realize that they're going to close the ride down right after he gets on and you were robbed of your turn at joy and excitement and living that kind of takes-your-breath-away kind of living because grief cut in. Right then, though, I tried to live in the sunny, bully-free moment.

I closed my eyes and smiled and said under my breath. "Good morning, sunshine."

"Well, good morning to you too." A deep, and masculine voice responded.

I opened my eyes as red spread down my face and neck like paint on a canvas. The man standing before me was the singer from last night. Lil's brother. The one that had made music that filled me with joy and sorrow all at once and he thought that I had called him "Sunshine." What a fool he must think me. I got nervous and then the words started…

"Oh, sorry. I'm sure your name isn't 'Sunshine,' is it? Unless your mother was a hippy but even then, it seems like a girl name don't you think? Maybe she called you 'Sunny' for short and then she got away with it. That wouldn't be so weird, right? I'm sure there are plenty of 'Sunny's' in this world. I just don't think you're one of them. If you are, that's no problem, though! It wouldn't make you any less masculine or anything. You're plenty masculine, believe me! I mean, whatever your name is, there's no doubting that you are most definitely, without a doubt, a man and a, umm, solid one at that. I don't mean that in an awkward way either!" I scrunched up my face in frustration before adding, "Sorry, I talk a lot when I'm embarrassed," I said through a deep, red hot flush of mortification.

"Does it help?" He asked. He was just standing there in front of me cool as a cucumber with a smile shining through his dark beard. He wasn't rattled by my embarrassing diatribe but he wasn't taking pleasure in it either. His eyes were soft and he seemed genuinely curious about whether or not blathering on like an idiot helped me feel less embarrassed.

I wanted to say "As if!" Like I was some teeny bopper from twenty years ago but I didn't.

"No, it definitely does not," I replied.

"Oh, well, that's too bad. I thought that maybe you had found the cure."

"Not yet. Still embarrassed over here."

"Well, let's juts fix that right up. Don't be embarrassed anymore," he said with a flourish of his hands.

"That's your cure? Just *don't* be?"

"Yes. Just realize that everyone has done things worthy of embarrassment so this is nothing out of the ordinary. You could have called me sunshine with your eyes *open*. Now that would have been worse."

"I guess you're right. Thank you for that, " I said with a laugh.

"Oh, it's the least I could do after making you cry last night."

My stomach sank and the embarrassment returned. He had recognized me then, had seen me retreat from the room in tears. Great.

"Oh no, you didn't make me cry. The song did. It just brings back some not so pleasant memories. You performed it very well, though. You performed all of the songs well! I truly was enjoying myself up until the end! It might have just been Lil's pot roast, though. I could eat that for every single meal if she'd let me."

"Well, her blueberry muffins aren't as good as the pot roast but they won't disappoint you either. What's your name by the way?"

"It's Willa Durham. And despite my unintentional name-calling earlier, I know your name isn't Sunshine. I think Drew told me it was Jake. Is that right?"

"Well, Jacob actually but I'll answer to Jake."

"So you and Lil both like to chop the names your parents gave you in half, then?" I asked.

"We just slice 'em and dice 'em! Speaking of Lil, I know she's got a big plate of breakfast and an even bigger pile of paperwork for you to go over. The breakfast will be enjoyable but the fun in that whole package stops there. Those books of hers are probably a mess. I'm going to escape while I can."

"Well, challenge accepted, Jacob! It was nice to meet you."

"You too, Willa. I hope your day has started better than yesterday's ended. Again, I'm so sorry."

"Thank you but no need. I'll survive." I gave him a smile and my best pistol pose which he returned with a smile and a nod. Somehow, with his kind eyes and easy smile, it was an affirmation that made me think that I actually just might survive here in this place, the one with the sunlight and food and people that were way too kind.

* * *

The morning rush had passed and I was sitting in Lil's office, a tiny closet of a space just off of the kitchen. She had said that I should work at the counter so I could be a part of the hustle and bustle but I had declined. I was starting to wonder if the counter was always where Lil worked on the business side of things. The records she kept seemed like they were recorded in the midst of quite a bit of hustle and bustle and the office bore very little sign of use. Even now, she had abandoned me to the files and folders while she was cooking up something that smelled like Heaven. I could hear her banging around in the kitchen humming something and then tapping her spoon on the metal mixing bowl in time with her song. I loved it from a distance but thought that the office, in it's underused, quiet, abandoned state was more my style.

The bookshelf on the wall opposite the door had a layer of dust thick and well settled on every inch except for a rectangular section that was about the size of the four binders that Lil had handed over that morning. The desk calendar in front of me hadn't been switched since St. Patrick's Day two years ago. I could see the beady little eyes of a leprechaun floating just under the date and his green hat behind my pile of work. I thought about ripping off the papers on the calendar to get it to the right date but then I realized that I could rip at it until it was gone and it still wouldn't catch up to real time. That calendar was from another year; the year Ollie died and I knew that it would never catch up to now. Just like my heart.

I could feel the melancholy nagging so I pushed the calendar down on its face so I couldn't see it anymore and turned my attention to the binders.

Jacob had been right. They were an absolute mess. Lil had warned me that this wasn't her strength and I was realizing that she had put it lightly. I had decided that the first thing I needed to do was to get her records from the last few years into some kind of organized fashion and then I would perform a full audit of the Aurora Boreal Inn and Café.

When I told Lil this plan she had said. "Do whatever you have to do to get things in shape honey. I just need to know what I've got and what I need. Drew is going to college next year. Numbers don't do much for me and we've always gotten by just fine doing the bare minimum as far as planning and organizing around here but now that he's looking into school, I think that the way that you see numbers will do a whole lot. A whole lot, Willa."

Drew had been there when she handed everything over to me and he had smiled at his mom while she talked.

"Mom, we don't even know where I'm going to school yet. Don't worry about the money."

"Drew, I'm not worried. I'm just planning. You'll go wherever you want because everywhere is going to want you. Did I tell you that he gets straight A's Willa?" She asked me.

"No, you didn't. That's great Drew!"

"Oh, it's nothing. I just like school is all."

"That's not all! He likes school and lacrosse and waiting tables around here. He's the most well-rounded boy you'll ever meet and schools are going to be lining up to take him. He wants to be a Doctor. A Pediatrician. That's why we need Willa to help us figure out what this place can crank out to send you." Lil smiled at Drew and I and I almost felt like we were in a huddle, game planning how we were going to send Drew into the end zone.

I liked it.

I thought about both of them while I made out dates written in Lil's swirled hand and put receipts and statements into the file system I had begun for myself. This was going to take a while but I didn't mind. I had nothing but time and I had done this before.

My mind raced back, past the date and the leprechaun on the

desk, past the heartache, past the tiny office I was in, to another one in Austin.

I let myself look at the picture in my mind, let myself turn it over and look at every detail, hear every word.

There was Ollie sitting at his computer. He was editing images from a senior photo shoot he had done that day, erasing the shy boy's shame pimple by pimple. He had only just started his photography business. He didn't know the beauty he would capture later on. And there I was, in jeans and a sweatshirt, studying for my CPA exam. I hadn't failed it yet. Hadn't taken it two more times and passed it.

We were so young, just putting our toes in the water of the careers we had started but we were there together. Just like always.

I could remember clear as day, Ollie looking up from his editing and smiling at me. Then he handed me a pile full of dog-eared contracts and bank statements and said, "Hey, you want a little practice? How about making sense of these and then giving me a statement on the state of my business?" He winked at me and kept up that smile that could get me to do anything.

"I need to study Ollie," I said smiling back.

"And I need an accountant."

"I'm not an accountant yet."

"Sure you are! You're the best in the business."

"And you're just too lazy to organize this stuff. You would much rather work on something beautiful. Like that." I smiled as I motioned to the framed portrait he had hanging in his office. It was a bride and groom, laughing as they leaned in for a kiss. Their noses were touching, they were so close to meeting lips but then they had laughed and their love was suspended in the air, floating between them; a love boat on waves of joy. It was loose and free and pregnant with promise in that moment right before they had sealed it all in with a kiss.

Ollie had captured that.

"Come on Willa, please? You know I'm not good at all the money stuff." He pulled me down onto his lap then and nuzzled my ear with a kiss.

"No, you aren't." I agreed as I giggled.

"But you are. You're good at everything I'm not, you know? That's how I know that you're my other half. You make everything I do whole."

I took the file. I put it all in order and I kept doing it from then on out. I kept making his work, his life whole and he did the same for me until he couldn't anymore. Until that day…

"Snack time!" Lil said as she floated into the office. She had a plate of cheese and crackers and grapes for me along with a smile on her lips and a furrow of concern in her brow.

"Everything alright?" she asked as she set the plate down right on top of the files I had been looking at.

I stared at it, its bright, rich colors arranged in a circle around the plate. The deep purple like a bruise next to the creamy, soft yellow of the cheese. Dark and light, deep and bright. The contrast of colors astounded me. The way that cheese and fruit were a commonly accepted perfect pairing as far as taste went but had they been left alone on the color wheel, they never would have touched. I wondered why life did that. Why did it have to take the dark and light and force them together, force them to coexist and get along? Why couldn't we just be left alone with all of the soft, thick, brightness of joy?

I grabbed a piece of cheese and popped it in my mouth, vowing to leave the grapes alone.

"Oh, I'm fine Lil. Just got lost in thought for a bit."

"What about?" She leaned on the desk and grabbed a piece of cheese and wrapped it around a plump, purple grape. Away it went into her mouth.

I looked down at the books and tried to think of how best to answer. I wasn't ready to tell her my story yet. I wasn't ready to introduce her to Ollie.

"Your books just reminded me of someone I used to work for. He was about as unorganized as you."

"What I'm hearing you say is 'he was a brilliant creative.' Then huh?" Lil said through bites of cheese and fruit.

I laughed a small laugh and said, "Yes, he certainly was."

"Well, I'm sure we would have gotten along well. I'll have to thank him someday for preparing you for this mess," she said with a smile on her lips.

My heart clenched at her words but I didn't want to start crying again while I explained that that would never happen.

"That would be nice," Is all I said. I looked down then before Lil could read further into my expression and started shuffling through a binder on the edge of the desk. I didn't know what I was looking for but I wanted to appear busy, to give my eyes something to focus on.

Lil watched me fumble around. She just stood there for a moment without moving or speaking or snacking. I could feel her eyes on me but I didn't feel like she was breathing down my neck. It actually felt almost like she was watching over me.

We remained like that for a minute or so, me pretending to work, her watching me with concern in her eyes, until I heard her open her mouth and draw in a breath like she was about to say something.

I looked up just in time to see her clamp her full lips shut, just in time to see something flash through her eyes. Was it sadness? Confusion? No, it was more like understanding. I watched her, waiting for the questions that usually came. The are "you alright?" "do you need to talk?"

Instead, she grabbed a length of my dark brown hair that was hanging over the front of my shoulder. She ran her fingers through it like my mother did when I was a girl and set it down gently on my back with a pat.

"I'll bring you some coffee Willa," she said. And then she left.

* * *

Lil did bring me that coffee right before the lunch rush started. It was as warm and comforting as it had been the day before and I was grateful for it. I was also grateful for the lunch rush. It gave Lil something to do other than checking on me and gave me the white noise of dishes clanging and people chattering that I needed to lose myself in my work instead of in my memories.

I stayed in that little office for the rest of the day, sorting through financial records and banks statements like my life depended on it. It wasn't a bad way to spend the day really.

I admire creativity and art a great deal but it confuses me equally as much. There's no rules, no laws set in stone. Everything that's already established is merely a suggestion, everything that has come before in your field of painting or music or whatever it is is to be valued and admired and then forgotten or changed. Artists are encouraged to bend and break whatever is established, to make it their own and then they're celebrated for it.

There's excitement in that. I love it as much as the next person. I appreciate it, really I do, but there's something scary about it too, something kind of frightening about the lack of stability and consistency. Everything is subjective. Everything is changeable. Where is the solid ground?

I noticed this about myself in high school. Others had known it about me far before that. Quinn could tell you story after story about how I thrived on routine as a kid, how I needed our parents to sing me the exact same two songs, give me a drink, and then feed my fish, Elvis and Costello, every single night in that order before I could even consider going to sleep. Friends could tell you how I was a strict rule follower, not even considering breaking curfew or underage drinking. Anyone could tell you that while some people see the world in shades of gray, Willa Durham sees the world in very clear black and white.

That's why, even after many passionate attempts, I was no good at anything artistic. I could never break out of the box, could never find a rule that needed breaking. That's why I chose Accounting. Because numbers always make sense. There's only one answer to arrive at and if you don't, you know you're wrong. But you're only wrong for a little while. Until you go back and find the wrong turn you took and fix it.

I love that about numbers. I love lining them up in perfect columns and rows like soldiers smart and gleaming, ready to face the enemy. That's how I saw my job. Like I was taking these concrete, dependable principles, and arming my clients with financial warriors to face their problems.

I had never come across an army as ragtag as Lil's books, though. They were as civilian as it got. Like the Colonial Army facing the British Regulars. Nothing was in order. There was no rhyme or reason and honestly, I didn't quite understand how she had made it this far.

It wasn't that the money wasn't there. It was obvious that she did take the time to make sure that money was in the bank and that taxes were paid but there was no planning, no uniform business model, no order to speak of and I absolutely loved it.

I could have kissed her for her mess and for inviting me in. This was going to take a while and I was grateful for the distraction.

Chapter 5

Jacob

I've seen plenty of women cry. Not because I'm some scumbag that makes them cry. I can see why you would think that based on how I started this whole thing but believe me, I do everything I can not to make them cry. Actually, I do everything I can to fix whatever feeling caused the tears.

I'm an Adolescent Psychologist with an emphasis in Music Psychology. There, that should clear it up.

I've seen plenty of females cry because I'm a psychologist and that's just what happens sometimes.

The tears come at unexpected times. They might be in the middle of telling me about their third-grade science fair or what their mom packed them for lunch that day and Bam! Tears.

There's nothing to be done to prepare yourself for them. I tell my patients that tears happen and that's just the way it needs to be. That's what my Dad used to tell me when I was a kid. He would see them welling up in my eyes and quietly say "Just let them fall, son. Clouds don't hold back the rain when it comes and neither should we. It all serves a purpose." And then he would pat me on the shoulder or pull me into a hug until it was all over and done with.

I know from both personal and professional experience that the problem comes when people try to stop the tears. When they hold them in and create a giant log jam of them because then, there's going to be a lot more at some point and it takes a lot longer to fix.

That's why I was glad when I saw her crying as she walked out. She looked like those tears had been an afterthought, like she almost forgot that she had a reason to cry but then they crept up on her like that feeling you get when you realize you've overslept.

That's it.

Before she had started crying, she had looked peaceful and happy but a little detached, like she was asleep in a room full of people that were awake. Like she was there and getting the rest that she needed but still not completely present like everyone else. She had smiled some, a small bewitching thing like a tiny flame dancing on the end of a match. She had even closed her eyes and swayed along to the music, just for a brief moment, a phantom of life within her.

I tried not to, but I think I watched her all night long.

And then the tears started and she was awake. She was feeling and hurting and drowning but awake and that was *good.*

I wanted to tell her that when I ran into her the next morning, that it was good that she had let herself wake up for a bit, but she looked like she had found rest again in the sunshine and in the laughter that comes from moments with new people. The conversation didn't wander that way and that was ok.

It just gave me another excuse to talk to her.

I didn't know why but I wanted to figure her out.

She had blended into the night with her dark brown hair and dark brown eyes and dark sadness that settled around her like the night sky around the moon but then, this morning, she had blended in with the day. She took sunlight in like a plant. Like she could perform photosynthesis and convert light into life. It showed through her smile with her straight white teeth and open hands with long tapered fingers. She was darkness and light all at once. She was the whole spectrum.

I wanted to know her stories; why songs made her cry and sunlight made her smile. She had a depth that drew me and a beauty that captivated me and it had been a long time since that had happened.

I thought about all of it as I walked the few blocks from the Café to my office. It had been so long since I had been interested in someone and I was trying to decipher the feelings I was having. I was trying to figure out if I wanted to encourage them.

I had to decide because it was my encouragement that had made the feelings smolder the last time. I had made them smolder like a bonfire and she had just been bewitched by the flames. I realize now that I was the only one that kept feeding the fire. She was just there, watching my love burn and warming herself with its heat. I realize now that she had kept that bucket of water close by the whole time, ready to dowse the flame when she got too hot. I was left shivering.

Did I want to risk that again?

My feet crunched the snow underneath me. There were only patches here and there in the places that the sun hadn't reached. That's the way it always was here in Colorado. Under the rays of the sun, the snow melted into water that ran down the sidewalks into the dead grass and the gutters, rushing to lend a hand to the work of growth and nourishment. But then there were always the spots in the shade or on the side of the street that the sun didn't reach where snow still lay. I knew that the spot across the street from my office would be there for days. It would collect the dirt and dust from cars passing by. The places that would be patted down by feet or cars parking on top of it would turn to ice.

In the shade, the winter lasted forever but where the sun hit, spring came every day.

I was sure that there was a metaphor there for a client so I pulled out my notebook from my messenger bag and wrote "Ice in the Shade", as neat as I could and stepped out of the shade and into the soggy, sun-soaked section of street in front of my office.

I felt its rays like a welcoming hug and smiled at its brightness. I knew it was cheesy and if Lil had been there with me, she would have laughed for days but I smiled and closed my eyes and said, "Good morning Sunshine."

* * *

"Angie, can you run out and get me some of Lil's coffee?" I called from my office. My assistant's desk was right outside my door but I had music playing and wasn't sure if she would be able to hear.

"I'm right here, Jake. No need to strain that perfect voice of yours." She appeared in my doorway with her arms crossed and one perfectly plucked eyebrow raised.

"Ok," I whispered. "Sorry! Can you run out and get me some of Lil's coffee?"

She rolled her eyes at me and smiled, batting the air with her palm like she was knocking my joke to the ground.

"Was that better?" I asked.

"Sure, boss," she said. She had been working for me for five years and had grown far too immune to my sense of humor. "I'll run over if you want but Drew just called and said that he's heading this way now. I'd be shocked if Lil didn't send some along with him."

"Oh, he is? Great! Did Drew say why he was coming?"

"Just asked if you had any open time on your schedule today and if he could fill it."

"Ok, well send him in when he gets here. In the meantime, this music is going right back on. Please don't shout over it ok?" I said in a mock lecture.

"I'll try my utmost," she said as she ducked out of the office with a flourish of her hands and a bow.

I laughed as I turned the music back up and that's how Drew found me.

"What's so funny Uncle Jake?"

"Oh hey, Drew! Nothing, just laughing at myself as usual. Come on in! How was school?"

"Good. I think I aced my history test so that's good. Lacrosse is starting back up soon too so I'm looking forward to that. Mom sent this over by the way." He set a plastic to-go cup full of coffee and paper bag full of something else on the desk in front of me. Judging by the smell, it was Lil's star shaped frosted sugar cookies. She said they were her tribute to Drew and me; stars because they used to be his favorite, sugar cookies because they were still mine.

"Lil knows me too well," I said as I took a sip of the steaming hot, perfect brew. "What else is new?" The room got quiet then. It wasn't like Drew and me to have any kind of extended silence, especially awkward silence but that's what we had. He shifted from one foot to the other, his tall, athletic frame seeming to try and fold in on himself.

He was embarrassed. It made me remember the time that I caught him singing at the top of his lungs on the stage in Lil's café to what he thought was an empty room. He was nine and he was mortified. When he was that young I just laughed it off with him, gave him a big bear hug and then sang in my goofiest voice to make him feel better. But here he stood, at seventeen, almost a man. I couldn't do that anymore.

I drew myself up and looked at him across my desk. "Hey Drew, what's up? Was there something you were wanting to ask me?"

He let all the air out of his lungs in one giant burst, causing his lips to flap together like a balloon opening as it flies across the room. I wanted to laugh again but knew better.

"Ok, here it is Uncle Jake. I want you to teach me how to play guitar."

I was taken aback a little. That was nothing to be embarrassed about.

"I'd love to Drew! I don't understand why you were nervous to ask me that, though."

"Oh, well, no reason!" he said as he sat down on the couch across from my desk. He picked at a button tuft on the arm trying to look nonchalant.

"Oh come on Drew. You're in my office. A psychiatrist's office, you really think you're going to pull one over on me. Why do you want to learn guitar?" I knew the answer before he said it and I smiled as I waited.

"Alright fine, it's for a girl."

"A girl huh?" I leaned back in my chair and put my hands behind my head. "Well, I can't think of any better reason. Let's get to it!"

"Really? That's it? No teasing or questions or anything like that?"

"Drew, I would never tease you about wanting to impress a girl with music. Why do you think I learned how to play?"

"You learned guitar for a girl too?"

"Sure did." Was all I managed. This was no time to tell him that young love fades, no time to wipe the hope off of his face that anything could happen with butterflies in your stomach and a guitar in your hands. He'd probably figure it out soon enough but at least he would have music to console him afterward.

I hated that I was assuming the worst for my own nephew but I told myself I was just being realistic. At least I didn't tell him what I was thinking. He would learn those lessons on his own and it would probably be good for him.

It had been for me.

"Drew, I'm happy to teach you, not only because music is the perfect weapon of choice when it comes to romantic conquest but because I think that music is a good weapon to have at any time. You'll need it all throughout your life."

Drew rolled his eyes at me and smiled. I knew he thought what I said was cheesy but I also knew that he was a wise enough kid to take it to heart too.

"Whatever you say, Uncle Jake. I just wanted a good way to ask Sophie to the prom but sure, that all sounds good too. When can we get started?"

"Well I have an appointment in about fifteen minutes and then I'll be finished up here for the day. How about I just hang around the Café after dinner tonight and we can start then?"

I thought going to the café was the best option. Then I could eat and give my lesson and maybe bump into Willa too…

"See you then, Uncle Jake!"

* * *

I got to the Café a few hours later, just as the dinner rush was picking up. Lil saw me walk in.

"Hey, brother! I saved your stool for you but you better hurry up and fill it before Hank over there convinces someone else to."

I walked over to the stool that Lil always put me in. Hank

Thompson was sitting in the one next to it and he pulled a face when I plopped down.

"What are you doing, Jake? I just about had a taker from that table over there."

I looked from Hank's bald head to his long, Santa-white beard that acted as a bib over his plaid shirt. It was like snow falling down and covering wrapping paper; plaid, flannel, wrapping paper. I followed his eyes to the table of women from the Senior Center sitting in the corner ensconced in a cloud of perfume, permed hair, and lipstick. I knew they came in every Wednesday to play bunko and that Hank came every Wednesday to watch them.

"Sorry, Hank. I can't argue with Lil. Why don't you just go pull up a chair with them? I like sitting by you every Wednesday but I think you would rather be over there," I said with a smile.

"Oh no, Jake, I couldn't go over uninvited. I'm a gentleman after all. I'll just make do with you again."

"Are you sure Hank? I think Mrs. Williams is eyeing you over her bifocals."

He swung around quicker than I thought his age would allow and blushed as red as his shirt as he accidentally made eye contact with Mrs. Williams. I chuckled right as Lil brought me a glass of water.

"You stop that, Jake. Mr. Hank will go over when he's good and ready and I'm sure he'll be greeted with a warm welcome. More coffee Hank?"

She filled his cup as the blush receded from his face and she and I smiled at each other.

"How was your day, Jake? Drew told me he stopped by."

I hesitated for a minute, not sure if Drew would want me to discuss the meaning of his visit with her. Not many boys wanted to talk about their love lives with their mothers. Not many people were Drew and Lil, though.

As if she read my mind and my hesitancy she said, "He also told me why. Isn't it the cutest thing?"

"It certainly is. I'm glad he told you. I wasn't sure if it was supposed to be private or not."

"Come on Jake, you know that boy can't keep anything from me! We're pals he and I!"

I smiled at my sister because she was absolutely right. She and Drew were thick as thieves and it did my heart good to see it.

"He should be done with his homework soon so you two can get started."

"There's no rush," I said.

I didn't necessarily want Lil to know that I was happy to hang around in hopes of catching a glimpse of Willa again. I had convinced myself that I had made her out to be prettier than she actually was over the course of the day. Lil would probably find out, though, probably see it all over my face if and when Willa walked in.

My thoughts must have jogged Lil's memory in some kind of weird brother-sister ESP thing because she said, "Excuse me for just a minute guys. Willa is still back in the office and I promised to bring her some dinner."

Before I could stop myself I said, a little too eagerly I might add, "She doesn't want to eat in there! Tell her to come out here and sit with all of us. There's a seat open right next to me."

Lil looked at me sideways and cocked her head a little bit. Her eyes narrowed ever so slightly and understanding shot through them. Just like that, I knew she saw right through me.

"Someday, Jake," Is all she said and then she disappeared into the kitchen.

I waited for Lil to return. Hank was good company for a few minutes, filling me in on his feed store in town and how business was. He had finished eating though and was slowly turning his attention back to the table of ladies. I had lost him. I was ready for Lil to come back, hopefully with my dinner and a temperament that was willing to answer a few of my questions.

She returned a few minutes later and both of my wishes came true.

"Here's your burger Jake. I added some extra pickles just like you like."

"Thanks, Sis. You always know."

"What do I always know?" she said with a twinkle in her eye.

"Well, just about everything. I can count on it really, that sixth sense of yours. I'm counting on it now."

"I think I know what you're referring to but I'll go ahead and ask; what do you need me to know all about for you?"

I looked at her straight on. I wasn't going to beat around the bush here. There was never any need for that with Lil. This was the person who used to build couch cushion forts with me and who waited up for me after my first date just to hear how it went. She knew me too well.

"Willa Durham." Is all I said. She would fill in the blanks with whatever she deemed necessary.

"Ahh, I see. Well, I know that she's beautiful but I think you know that too."

I didn't say anything, just popped a French fry into my mouth and smiled.

"Right. I know that she is smart. Really smart because she's making sense of all that back there. I know that she just got here and I think she's planning on staying because that's her trailer full of stuff in the parking lot. Oh, and I know that she takes her coffee black."

"So you like her then." I knew Lil's theory about black coffee.

"I do!"

"What else?" I asked between bites of burger.

"Well, the rest I'm still trying to figure out. I don't know the details but if my heart is right, that woman is hurting. She's hurting really bad and doesn't really know how to find her way out of it. I think that might be why she came here. So, naturally, I'm going to do everything I can to help her feel better."

"Naturally," I said with a laugh. That was Lil. She saw right to the heart of everyone and then did everything in her power to nurture and love whatever was there. She was a mother to anyone that would let her be.

Lil leaned on the counter and looked at me with a squinty, discerning look. She stared at me like that for a minute and then a great big smile broke across her face. She said. "I think you will too."

"I will what?"

"Help her feel better. I have to go check on some tables," she said. She flicked a towel over her shoulder, turned and kicked her leg up behind her, teasing me. She just loved to keep me in the dark.

As I finished my burger, I thought about what Lil said. She really hadn't told me anything I didn't know. Her information was cursory at best but I thought about it all the same. Especially the part about Willa being sad. Last night had told me as much.

If that was where she was at, I would probably do well to leave her alone. Healing was different for everyone and I didn't want to be the undoing of anything for her. Sure she was pretty but I could just leave it at that. It was better this way anyway.

I didn't want end up in the place that she was at again, hurting and alone. I had been there before…

Before my memories could take a turn on my mind's stage, Drew came bounding down the stairs and into the café.

"Hey Drew, perfect timing!" I said. "Ready to head upstairs?"

He reached down and grabbed one of the two guitars I had lugged over with me in one hand and a few of the fries I had left on my plate in the other.

"You were finished with those right?" he asked mid-bite.

I laughed and said. "Sure."

"Ok well let's get started! I'm so pumped!"

We started walking towards the stairs as he chattered on about the different songs he was debating on using to ask Sophie to prom.

"...or maybe you might have a better idea. I don't want it to be too hard because I want to play it from memory, just walk up to her in the cafeteria in front of everyone and start playing! Won't that just be epic? It's totally sappy and stuff like girls like. Hey, Willa!"

I hadn't noticed it but we had walked right past Lil's office. The door was open and there was Willa, with a bite suspended in mid-air. She blushed a little at being found like that but her eyes brightened too.

"Hey, Drew! How was school? Oh, and Jacob! Good to see you again too."

Without giving it permission my heart flip flopped a little when she said "Jacob". For some reason, it sounded good on her voice.

Before I could answer Drew said, "It was good. Just school. I don't mean that in a bad way cause I like school I just mean nothing really that big happened. Maybe tomorrow. Hey, it's after six o'clock, you should stop working," he said with a shrug and a smile.

"Oh, I don't mind. It gives me something to do," she said.

"Well, if you want something to do, you could come upstairs and sit in on my guitar lesson. My Uncle Jake is teaching me!"

"Drew, you are the most confident kid I know! I would never have invited someone to come hear me fumble around on the guitar."

"Do you play?" I asked.

She looked at me then and again, that blush stole over her cheeks. "Oh no! I'm sure I would be awful at it!"

"Oh come on! I bet not! You should try sometime! I bet Uncle Jake would teach you too." Drew said.

I looked at her sitting in the chair, her legs crossed like a lady sitting with the Queen, her long eyelashes fanning out over her cheeks as she looked down, demurring to Drew's encouragement. She was femininity itself and I had to stop myself from giving Drew's suggestion a hardy "Of course I would!"

Thankfully she spoke up before I could. "Maybe some other time. You guys just enjoy your lesson and I'll enjoy listening through the floorboards."

"Alright, then but could you do one thing for me?"

"Sure Drew!" she said.

"Could you come up with a few songs you think are kind of romantic? I'm doing all this so that I can ask a girl to the Prom by singing to her. It would be nice to have a girl's point of view on it."

She smiled at Drew but the beautiful crescent didn't reach up to her eyes. It was like the moon hanging too close to the earth. She cleared her throat and shook her head like she was trying to shake something off and said, "Sure Drew! Every girl deserves a guy who thinks like you do. I'll put my best, most romantically inclined brain cells on it."

"Thanks!" he said. "Ok well, we better get to it, Uncle Jake! By Willa!"

"By you two!" she said with a smile.

I stood there a second longer trying to find something to say to her. Our only interactions had included her being mortified that morning and then this where I had only managed to come up with one stupid question to ask her. I didn't know why it mattered. I didn't know why I cared because I had just decided that I wasn't going to pursue her, but mattered it did.

"I'm sorry I keep sneaking up on you." I finally said.

"Oh, no need to apologize. I don't mind. I don't really know anyone around here so I'm happy to make friends in any way possible," she said with a shrug and a smile.

"Well ok then. Enjoy your evening friend." I said with a nod and then ducked out of the doorway, her smile hot on my trail.

Chapter 6

Jacob

My mom left us when I was three.

Every time I say that, I feel like it should make me feel more. I know it's a pretty big deal. I mean, I grew up without a mother, without even many memories of her. I can recall a few things here and there; waves of red hair, cascading down as she picked me up, the way her voice sounded like deep, rich chocolate when she sang me to sleep. It's all fuzzy but I have those few things.

Then she left and the memories trailed off and we became a family of three.

I've never understood it really. I haven't resented her or hated her, just haven't understood it. When I see Lil with Drew, the way that her heart revolves around him and how she would give up her very breath so he could have it, I wonder how a mother could leave her kids. Especially one that begot a daughter like Lil, who mothers so completely and perfectly. All of us were confused by it but my

Dad was always able to explain it away.

"Your mother is like the wind." He would tell us. "On the good days, she brings refreshing and breath and life but then, the wind can't stay can it? It's always moving, always forcing itself away. Try to understand you guys. It's not that she doesn't love you, it's that her nature keeps her from standing still."

It didn't make sense to me then what he meant by "her nature". Later, Lil and I learned it was a veiled euphemism for the mental illness that she battled. That, combined with a little bit of selfishness but my Dad would never say that. He never spoke a word against her even though we saw the hurt in his eyes from time to time.

No, instead he filled up all of the space that she had left in our lives by taking on her role. I'm sure it kept him distracted but it also filled our void.

He learned how to French braid Lil's thick, curly hair and he probably pined for our mother with every stroke of the brush. So like her is Lil. He learned how to make grilled cheese just like I liked; cut in triangles with the crust cut off. He filled in at every school or sporting event, the man in a sea of women. The father among mothers.

He did it all, my dad and we honestly never felt much of a void. He was enough. He really was. He could be soft the way that a mother can and he could be strong like a father. He could make us laugh and hold us when we cried, he had patience, he had grace, he had strength, and most of all, he had love like I've never seen love before.

I remember one Christmas morning when I was nine or ten I woke up before Lil did. It was early, the sun hadn't risen yet and that cozy quiet that lingers just before dawn was settled into our house. It was Christmas morning though and that alone gives kids permission to wake up, not sunlight. Lil was long past believing in Santa but I was still a disciple of the Christmas myth and wholeheartedly believed. I woke up because I had heard something downstairs and had thought that this was my chance to get a glimpse of him.

I took the stairs one at a time, touching each with only my tippy toes careful to avoid the spots that I knew squeaked. I knew that if Santa saw me out of bed before the sun was up, he would be disappointed in me and that was a heartbreak that I simply couldn't bear. I finally reached the bottom step and turned towards the living room where our tinsel-strewn tree stood next to the fireplace. I held my breath as I turned, expecting to see something that I would never forget, that I could hold out to Lil as proof that she was foolish to defect from the Christmas cause but what I saw was something different altogether.

It was my Dad.

He was hunched over a brand new bike for me, the one that I had cut out of the catalog and mailed to the north pole. He was filling up the tires and tightening the gears. He was still wearing his sweater and tie that he wore to the Christmas Eve service at church the night before. His eyes were red-rimmed from lack of sleep and his brow was furrowed as he concentrated on his task but his face smiled as he worked.

The knowledge that Santa wasn't real began to sink in but before despair could follow on its coattails, something else filled my mind. Santa wasn't real but my Dad was.

He had probably done every single Christmas of our entire lives; made magic and memories. He had done everything he could to carry it on and to make it perfect and he had done it without the help of elves or reindeer or my mom. That was more magical than any Christmas fairy tale I had ever heard.

I watched him there, in the living room working on my bike by the light of the Christmas tree in his clothes from the night before and even at that age, I knew that he was amazing. Something about that picture made me realize how strong he was. The load he carried as a single parent was heavy and cumbersome. It required him to carry us, all three of us, 24/7 yet he did it with a smile on his face.

I sat there on the stairs, watching him through the railings on the banister until he noticed me and his face fell as the blood drained out of it.

"Hi Buddy," he said. "I just came down here because Santa came by a little bit ago but he was running a little behind so he asked me to put the finishing touches on your present. He came upstairs and got me and everything. If you look close enough, you'll probably be able to see the snow he tracked in and…"

"Dad," I interrupted. "It's ok. I know he's not real."

"Oh buddy," he sighed. "I'm so sorry. I'm sorry I was too loud. I ruined it for you." His face fell and he dropped the wrench he had been using onto the carpet as he shifted his weight off of his haunches and sat cross-legged on the floor.

"No, you didn't Dad!" I told him. I walked over to him and sat in his lap. "Sure Santa's not real but you know what? You're better than Santa. You're my Dad."

He laughed then and hugged me tight, a feeling that was far better than Christmas morning or my birthday or anything else good in the world.

"Yeah son, I'm your Dad and that's the best thing I'll ever get to be."

"Thanks, Dad."

"For what?"

"For the bike and for, well everything. You just do everything." I said with a shrug.

And he did. He *did* everything and he *was* everything to me. He was my best friend, my hero, my father, my mother, my example, my Christmas…

So when he died ten years later, I finally realized what it felt like to learn that Santa isn't real. Your innocence and your dreams and your faith and hope, the best thing you have as a kid is shattered. What do you cling to then?

* * *

It had been a week since I had met Willa and I still couldn't shake the desire I had to spend time with her. I had tried to convince myself that the timing wasn't right, that I wasn't right or she wasn't right but still, the attraction lingered and I was weary from fighting it. I wanted to avoid her altogether but the truth was, I was at the Café a lot and so was she. So, I resigned myself to the use of self-control and the hope that time would tamper the crush that was developing.

Developing it was, though.

She was beautiful. That was something that science couldn't even deny but the mystery surrounding her and her obvious need for *something* called out to me. The force that comes over a man when attraction and mystery are combined is a powerful pull but I hoped that I could be stronger.

I had seen the damage that could come from forcing a relationship when the timing wasn't right and it had been enough to make me quite relationships altogether. I had been content with the idea that I wouldn't ever actively pursue that kind of thing again but now this thing with Willa had come over me and it was kind of disturbing.

I tried not to think about her but there she was, right in front of me.

I sat on the stage of the cafe with the rest of my band rolling up our sound chords and Willa, Lil and Drew were the only people left in the room after our show at the Aurora Boreal Inn and Cafe. I glanced at her any chance I could get.

She wasn't watching me.

She sat at a table in the middle of the room with her laptop open and a cup of tea beside her, working. Her brow furrowed just slightly as she concentrated and I could see her mouthing her thoughts silently, talking to herself without any sound.

I wanted to know what she was thinking, what message she was conveying to herself and somehow, drop my name into the mix.

"Are you almost done with that Jake?" It was Mike, our drummer. He was waiting not so patiently for the chord that I was rolling so he could put it in the bag and pack up our equipment. He owned a moving company in town so he had access to a trailer that he hitched to the back of his pickup that we used to store all of our gear in between shows. It was nice of him to do and I felt bad that I had been holding him up with my staring and daydreaming.

"Oh, yeah sorry Mike. I know you need to get home to Janelle and the baby. Here you go." I said.

"Thanks, Jake. And by the way, staring won't do you any good. Just go talk to her."

I laughed a little at his comment. He was right of course but I wasn't going to bite.

"I think I'll just keep watching from afar for now buddy. Thanks, though."

"Come on Jake. She seems nice enough. Smart. Obviously pretty. Why not try?"

I looked at him for a second and held his gaze and then looked down at my hands, pretending to study the callouses on my fingertips from my guitar strings.

"Oh, I see. Are you still hung up on that? Jake, the time's going to come where you'll have to finally leave that in the past and move towards your future." He clapped me on the shoulder and gave it a squeeze. "Why can't it be today?"

I watched him walk out with Emmet, our bass player, waving

goodbye as they took the last load of stuff to the trailer. We had been friends for almost ten years now, forged by the bond of music and the simple fact that life happens and the people that are there with you through it become more and more important with each event. We had been through college, grad school, marriages, babies, break-ups, deaths in the family, and about a hundred Denver Broncos games. Those things were as good as glue. They knew me almost as well as Lil. Well enough to get away with pushing me forward. I wasn't quite ready to let the force move me, though. Maybe someday, but not today.

I shook my head and clapped my hands together, forcing myself to make a clean break with the train of thought I had been on. The sound was a little louder than I expected though and it made Lil, Drew, and Willa jump.

"Sorry," I said sheepishly. "Drew, should we head upstairs for your lesson?"

"Why go upstairs?" Lil asked as she wiped down a table in the corner. "Just stay here. Willa and I could use a little music while we work right Willa?"

Willa looked up, obviously startled by the fact that Lil had involved her in the conversation.

"Couldn't hurt," she said with a half smile before she turned back to her laptop.

She was completely uninterested. In me and the music.

"Sure, ok," I said looking at her for half a second too long. Lil saw me and watched with understanding in her eyes. She didn't say anything. Just looked and a million stories and words passed between us.

Drew walked up to the stage and sat on a stool next to me, picking up my extra acoustic guitar. Actually, it wasn't my "extra" guitar. It was the first guitar I had ever known. The one that I had learned on, the one that had been held by the hands that taught me everything else in life.

"Drew, you know that was your Grandpa's guitar don't you?" I asked him while I showed him how to tune it.

"I thought so," he said cheerily. "I've seen him holding it in the picture on your desk. It's the same picture that Mom has on her nightstand."

I knew exactly what picture he was talking about. It was taken one summer night that we had spent with friends. Lil and I were teenagers and we were huddled around our Dad while he sat in a lawn chair with his guitar over his lap. It was a moment frozen in time, one taken between songs sung around a fire pit, between bites of 's'mores and laughs and hugs. It was a sticky moment, like melted marshmallow in my mind and it clung with its sweetness and warmth. We smiled back at the camera, all three of us with the same identical grin. It was perfect and I knew that Lil felt the same.

"He taught me on that old thing and now I'm teaching you. He would have been so excited about that." I said with a smile.

"That's so perfectly and poignantly special." Willa's voice floated to us on a whisper from her table. I looked up, surprised that she had been listening.

"I'm sorry if I'm eavesdropping but I overheard what you said and I think that's beautiful. What a gift you're giving him, Jacob," she said with a smile that filled her whole face and bridged the gap between us.

"I agree completely!" Lil said with tears in her eyes. "A gift." She smiled a small smile and as her cheeks moved up from the effort of it, a single tear rolled down her cheek.

"Well, I don't remember much about Grandpa but I'm pretty sure he'd rather we just get to it instead of crying, Mom. Am I right Uncle Jake?" Drew said as he pulled the guitar out of my hands.

"You are Drew," I said with a laugh. "Ok, let's get started. I was thinking and I decided that it's best if you stick with the classics for this Prom thing. What about learning 'The Way You Look Tonight' Drew?"

"If you think so Uncle Jake but I've got to be honest, I don't know what song you're talking about."

"What?" Came Willa's voice, full of passion and surprise. She had slammed her computer closed at Drew's admission and looked at us with big eyes. "Oh Drew, you have to know that song. It's a must, an absolute, a sort of prerequisite to feeling any kind of romance at all!" She looked down at her hands and paused. A far away look filled her eyes for a breath of a moment and then she shook her head, pushing aside whatever had snagged her train of thought. Her voice returned with forced brightness and she smiled a pasted on smile. "You're going to love it, Drew. It's a perfect suggestion, Jacob. Excuse my cutting into your lesson. I'm so sorry."

"No need to apologize," I said calmly smiling at her. "I think you made my case for me better than I could have." Was all I said. What I wanted to say was that I completely agreed with her and was oddly excited by the fact that she loved that song as much as I did.

"Well, I'm sure you're wrong. You're the musician here so you probably know better than I do that the song is a classic in every form. I don't know much about the musicality of it all but I just love the words. The idea of cherishing a moment so fiercely, of capturing it so vividly in your mind that you can look back on it years later and find the same amount of awe and wonder and joy and, well, love in it as you did the first time it happened. That's special you know? Memories are all that last…" She trailed off then but the passion that had filled her voice now filled the room.

She was right of course. Completely right and I smiled at her.

"Well Willa, I think you're quite the nostalgic."

"For better or worse," she said with a shrug. "Really, I'm so sorry for cutting into your lesson. Please, go on."

I smiled at her one more time just to reassure her that her thoughts were welcomed here and then I began to show Drew the fingering of the chords that were in the song. He took to it pretty quickly just as I suspected he would and we ran through them a few times.

"Ok, now what I want you to do is to try and follow along with me. I'm going to play the song and you try and keep up. I'll play at a slower tempo to make it easier ok?"

"Let's do it!" Drew said.

I began strumming, softly nodding to Drew and announcing the next chord change as they came. He kept in step with me well and we played our duet, me with my guitar, him with my father's.

I sang the words softly letting the softness of them float between Drew and I. They always gave me a sense of longing and peace all at the same time. I guess that's what classics do. I wasn't paying too much attention to the vocals, just enough to keep Drew on pace with the song, to teach him the melody and eventually, he started to hum with me.

Music came naturally to him just like everything else he did.

We looped through the song over and over again, giving him a chance to learn through repetition and eventually, he had learned the tune well. Well enough that I jumped up and sang harmony to his melody. I smiled at him while we sang. It was lilting and soft but it was strong enough, easy enough to give him the confidence he needed. Lil began cheering for us, her mouth a smile with sound attached and Drew laughed through his singing, fumbling on the guitar ever so slightly. I nodded at him to keep going and gave him a little wink to reassure him.

Then I looked over at Willa.

She was smiling from ear to ear while she stared at her computer. I guessed she was trying to give Drew a little privacy, the comfort of knowing that every set of eyes wasn't on him while he learned, but she was listening and listening well. And she was enjoying it.

We kept singing, *I* kept singing if only to keep her happy.

Her eyes, the ones that still harbored sadness in the depths but a smile on the surface raised just slightly and grazed the plane above her computer. They found mine and our gaze locked for a second.

She nodded from me to Drew as if she was saying "he's getting it!" and then she looked down, right before the next phrase came, suddenly shaking her head and letting her smile fade. Squinting at the computer screen and feigning interest in her work once again.

I sang the last lines of the chorus, but without her looking up, without the shield of her eyes guarding me and distracting me from my memories the words felt flat. I didn't want to let them conjure memories of what I thought love was. I Looked at her closely and by the light of her computer screen, I could tell that for Willa, the words were becoming knives and torches and clubs that knocked down her smile. She had gone from joy to sadness again like she was jump roping over the line between them.

It was time to wrap this up.

We pushed the song on towards the end and Lil and Willa both clapped when it was over. They were proud and we could tell.

"All I have to say is, I better start saving my money for prom because Sophie is not going to be able to say no to that," Drew said jokingly.

"Well if she does, you can take me," Lil said as she walked up and kissed him on the cheek. "I'm so proud of you, Drew!"

"It was lovely!" Willa finally said. "Both of you." I was surprised at her praise and blushed while I looked down and studied the floor.

"Thanks, Willa!" Drew told her. "I better get up to bed everyone. I have to be at school early for weight training."

"Ok, Drew. Night buddy!" I told him.

"I think I'll turn in too," Lil said. "Jake, just lock up as you go ok?"

"Oh, I better follow you up too then huh?" Willa said nervously as she rushed to shut down her computer. She was obviously uneasy about being alone with me.

"No rush Willa, finish your tea, take your time!" Lil said, and when Willa wasn't looking, she winked at me. Then she rushed up the stairs before we could protest.

I rolled my eyes.

There was nothing to be done but to be there together. I had to put my gear away and she had been socially roped into staying and chugging down her lukewarm tea. She began taking large gulps of it and looking around awkwardly.

"Willa, I can tell you'd rather be upstairs. I won't tell Lil If you don't drink every last drop." I said as I put away my guitar. I hoped my tone was light and kind instead of the way I actually felt; irritated that I wanted her to stay and irritated that she didn't want to.

"Oh no, it's fine. I'll stay. I have to get my stuff put away anyway," she said in a tone that was full of forced brightness. Like fluorescent light or those fake candles with the battery operated flames.

"It's ok if you don't want to be alone with me," I said directly.

"Oh, it's not that. I don't feel uncomfortable around you or anything. It's just that, well, I'm kind of embarrassed."

"Embarrassed?" I said with a laugh. "Why?"

"Because, whenever I'm around you, I say or do things that are overly dramatic or emotional and you probably think I'm just the most ridiculous woman you've ever had to listen to," she said in a flurry of words and hand movements followed by another gigantic gulp of tea.

"Willa, I promise you I don't."

"Well, why not? I think that I am," she said emphatically.

"You think that you are around me? Ridiculous or dramatic?" I asked her calmly

"No, all of the time. The truth is that I'm just generally dramatic about things when it comes to emotions. Both in good ways and bad. I just usually can mask it around strangers for a while. You somehow bring it all out all of the time." She sighed and set her cup down.

"I think that's good. Be who you are. All of the time. People can love it or hate it but they can deal with it. I happen to enjoy talking to you. I wouldn't call it being dramatic, though. I'd call it passion and that's something that's in short supply with most people."

"Oh, well, thank you then I guess," she said surprised. "I'll try and remember that the next time I'm berating myself for something I've done. I'll just call it passion."

I smiled and nodded, as I picked up my guitar to leave. "Glad I could help cheer you up. Honestly, though Willa, it's ok to feel what you feel and to be who you are. Never worry about that around me. I like it all. Have a good night."

And with that, I left her standing with her cup of tea in her hand and a smile on her face. I was proud of myself really. I had said just enough but not too much and when I went to bed that night, I finally could imagine that at least a friendship could begin with Willa.

That would have to be enough for now though because I wasn't ready to begin clinging hard to sand again. I couldn't see every piece of me fall through the cracks of my heart like they did before.

But her smile that shone at me from behind her computer haunted my dreams and I knew this thing wasn't over yet.

Chapter 7

Willa

I woke up and pulled back the curtains in my room to see a giant pillow of white covering the ground beneath me. It seemed as if that very ground had been raised up to meet me, inch by inch over the long, cold night, each flake had piled high on the others until, ever so slowly, the ground and my window were closer.

I grabbed a sweatshirt from the closet and walked back over to the window. I loved watching the flakes fall so beautifully, so gracefully from the sky, each twirling and cascading down their own path until they all landed together. I guessed that there were about two feet of snow outside and every inch of it fascinated me. The way that tiny little flakes, full of intricacies that my naked eye would never know could combine forces with other tiny little flakes and take over the world before me? It enchanted me.

In my trance like state standing hypnotized by snow before my window, I supposed that this was my baptism, that I had lost my old self completely in this winter wonderland. I had laid my body down on my bed last night like a person backing down into the water and awoken to this. This fresh, new, sparkly, beautiful thing and I was fresh and new because of it. I was falling in love.

The moment was peaceful, serene. I pictured myself standing like this, like a painting on a postcard. There I would be, ensconced in brush strokes and coziness with some flowery saying written above my head. Something like "Warm Greetings from Cold Colorado." Or "Let it Snow!" It was a nice thought and I breathed in the peaceful moment until all of the sudden, I heard a loud "Thud! Thud! Swoosh!" sound on the roof above my head.

Before my mind could catch up to the sound, the bottom of a sled appeared in my view. A sled with Drew on top of it. He flew over the eaves above my window out, out, out until he landed with a soft thud in a snow drift below. He glided down the sloping lawn for a few seconds and then came to a slow stop yards away from my window. The virgin snow before me bore a long, straight track pointing to Drew, jumping up with his hands in the air.

I could hear his muffled voice through the window panes saying "That was awesome! Ok, your turn!"

I wondered who he was talking to but I wasn't left guessing for long. Not two seconds after he called up towards the roof, I heard Lil's voice loud and full of excitement.

"Ready or not, here I cooooooome!" There was the same "Thud, Thud, Swoosh," and then another sled with a jet stream of red, curly hair flying out behind it. She landed, making her own tracks in the snow until she stopped just short of Drew. She got up and he walked over to her and they high fived before dissolving into laughter.

It was a moment that was so warm, so full of love and life that I thought it would melt the snow right out from under their feet.

I laughed with them, once again moved by their bond and their lust for life. They saw me then and waved furiously up at my window, motioning for me to open it to them, to the wonderland before me.

I slid it open, relishing the cold air on my face.

"Morning!" I said and I watched my words go to them in a puff of warm air in the cold.

"Morning Willa! I hope we didn't wake you up!" Drew yelled to me.

"Not at all, I was just enjoying a peaceful winter wonderland until you two crazy people flew right into it!"

"Crazy is one way to put it," Lil said. "I like to call it fun! I laid out some extra snow gear for you in the office! Get out here!" She motioned at me with her gloved hand, inviting me out. Inviting me in.

"Maybe later," I said with absolutely no intention of ever following them onto that roof. "I'm not dressed yet."

"Well get to it!" Lil yelled. "We've got a snow day on our hands and there's no time to waste!"

* * *

An hour later, Lil and Drew trudged their way back inside the café, leaving zigzagged patterns of snow from the bottom of their boots on the welcome mat. I was waiting for them at the counter, dressed in a cozy cashmere sweater and jeans. Lil had laid out muffins, fruit, and coffee for everyone before she went on her high-flying sledding adventure with Drew and I had happily found them when I came downstairs.

"I'm glad you found the food, Willa! Fill up so we can get on with our fun." Lil said with a smile and a wink.

"I'm having my fun right now Lil. There's not much better in this world than eating your food." I said with a smile between bites.

"Well, that's easy to say when you haven't been out flying,"

Drew said. He grabbed a blueberry muffin and ate half of it in one bite.

"Flying huh? Is that what you call it?"

"That's what we named it, yeah."

"You and your mom?" I asked.

"No, me and Uncle Jake. Back when I was little I used to ride on the sled with him and we would fly off of the roof like that whenever there was a big snowstorm."

"It nearly killed me with worry until Jake talked me into doing it myself. Now, it's an Aurora Boreal Inn staple! You'll see."

"What do you mean?" I asked in confusion.

"She means that everyone should be here soon," Drew said with a twinkle in his eye.

I looked from one to the other. There they went again, sharing that ornery look of theirs with their identical smiles and flashing eyes. "Oh, you two! Why don't you just tell me already!" I said in mock exasperation.

They both laughed, giving definition to the term "peels of laughter", like each note of joy that came from them was an orange peel pulling back to reveal juicy, nourishing life. It was as if it was filling the room with the aroma of citrus and sunshine. It was Vitamin C for the soul, that laughter was.

"Alright, we'll stop with the teasing Willa," Drew said. "What we mean is, anyone within walking distance of the Inn should be here soon so they can fly too. It's a blast! You'll see! The coffee seems low Mom. I'll go fill it up."

Within fifteen minutes, their prophecy came to life.

A steady trickle of people flowed in through the front doors, covered in puffy snow pants and coats, gloves and hats, thick, sturdy, clompy boots. All with sleds in hand.

I didn't recognize everyone but most people were familiar. There were the sisters that ran the flower shop a few blocks up the road. They lived above it with one of their daughters. I wasn't sure who's because both of them held that maternal glow like a candle in their eyes when they looked at her. There was the family of five that lived in the 1920's bungalow across the street and there was Hank, good old Hank who didn't need a scarf because of his long, snow-white beard. I wondered how he would find the energy to climb up on the roof and sled down but something told me that he would.

Then there was Jake, coming in behind all of them, carrying a bright red sled and his guitar. He just smiled watching the neighborhood mingle with the few guests that the inn had, smiled watching Lil host them. Then he smiled at me, sitting at the counter holding my cup of coffee. Warmth filled me and I didn't let myself wonder if it was from the look he was giving me or the warm brew I was sipping on. I took another sip just in case.

It had to be the coffee.

He made his way over to me, winding through the thin path that was allowed between bulky snow gear, sleds, and excitement.

"Happy snow day, Willa!" he said in his deep, quiet, joyful voice.

"Happy snow day to you too, I guess. Is a snow day like a holiday around here?" I asked.

"Sort of," he said with a shrug. "You have to remember that I work with teenagers so I tend to get excited about things on their level. A day off of school and work is something of a holiday." His tone was kind of self-deprecating and light. "Plus, snow tends to bring the neighborhood together here and that kind of feels like Christmas too, all of us being together."

He looked around at the café, filling up with people and there was contentment in his eyes.

"There is something special about today." I acknowledged. "I've never seen anything as beautiful as that sparkly snow covering the mountains. Or as beautiful as Lil and Drew smiling at each other in it."

He laughed at me. "I suppose there is a kind of beauty to their joy. It's unfiltered and unique, isn't it? Special."

That was part of it but not all of it. There was more to their bond, something stronger, like an undercurrent in the ocean, churning below the surface strong and hard, keeping the water on top fresh and moving. Their joy, their connection was as steady and strong as the ocean's tide.

"I've never seen a mother and son quite like them." I finally said. "They belong to each other, don't they? Their souls are connected."

Jake looked at me, his eyes soft below the rim of his winter hat. It was as if a million memories and feelings were falling down within them, like snow falling to the ground. "They do. They are. You should ask Lil how they got that way sometime," he said.

He poured himself some coffee and looked at me, urging me to do what he said with his eyes. There must have been some kind of importance to the story, something he thought I needed to hear.

"Maybe I will," I said.

"I hope you do Willa. Everyone has a story that someone needs to hear. Now, are you going to fly with us today?" He changed the subject so abruptly that I almost missed the urgency behind his words. Almost but not quite. I decided to make a point of talking to Lil soon.

I followed Jacob's question though and tried to find the best answer for him.

"I'm not too sure," I said.

"Oh come on, why not?"

"Why not? Because I don't want to break my neck that's why!" I said with a laugh.

"Oh Willa, we've been doing this for years and no one has gotten hurt yet. The odds are in your favor."

The odds. The odds had been in my favor before too. It wasn't likely that I would have to bury my fiancé before his thirtieth birthday but I did. The odds were that I would be married now but I wasn't. The odds were nothing to trust in my opinion.

"Well, with my luck, I would be the first person to defy those odds and I have no interest in that, thank you very much," I told him.

"Well, you can stay in here by yourself as long as you want but the party will be outside. Nothing ventured nothing gained, Willa. I hope you'll join us." His words were simple yet steady. He wasn't trying to twist my arm, just stated his case and then walked outside with everyone else.

And just like that, the back door closed and I was alone inside the café.

I could hear the laughter outside, the swoosh of the sled on the roof and the cheers of everyone as each person took flight and then landed in the snow. I watched them through the window as they stood out in the freezing cold with snowflakes swirling around them.

Not one of them shivered, though. Some huddled close, hugging each other to their sides as they watched. Drew ran around with the other kids, younger and older, throwing snowballs at each other not in a way that tried to conquer or harm. It was more like they were blowing kisses; big wet, soft, cold kisses that landed on the backs or arms of coats and splattered into a million pieces. It was a game in every sense and Drew was the ringleader of it all. He was hosting. He was leading. He was filling the yard with fun and laughter.

There was life out there in that frozen world and while I sat in the warm, cozy café, I shivered.

Was this what I wanted? To live in the shadow of grief? To let the one time that the odds hadn't been kind to me keep me isolated and alone?

I had a vague sense of the fact that I was having a self-reflective moment. I knew I was being introspective, that there was a metaphor in the fact that everyone else was happy and living outside my window and that I was willingly choosing to stay inside with nothing but muffins and chairs to keep me company. I also knew that the obvious answer should be no; I don't want to live like this.

I didn't have some overwhelming need to change boil up inside of me, though. There was not this moment of realization where I pulled my heart up by the bootstraps because I knew it was time to move one. I didn't go grab a sled like I was picking up a firearm to go off and fight some epic battle with loneliness and grief.

I wasn't stirred. I wasn't impassioned. My heart was still sad, content to be inside all alone.

My head was beginning to travel, though. I could picture myself outside flying down that roof. I thought it might be good for me. I knew that if Ollie was here, he would be out there leading the charge so I probably would have gone too.

I knew it. I just didn't feel it.

Sometimes, the knowing just has to be good enough, though. Sometimes, all the time really, our hearts move at a different pace than our heads and there are times when our heads have to be in charge.

This was one of them.

I grabbed my coat, pulled on the fluffy winter gear that Lil had laid out for me, and I headed outside into the blinding white light of warmth and companionship.

* * *

I was on a roof. Holding a sled on a roof.

I was out of my mind.

I must have been, right?

To be up on the top of a roof, preparing to slide down and fly into a drift of snow? That was crazy!

Somehow, Lil had talked me up there, she had stood at the bottom of the ladder, a plug stopping my insides from pouring down the rungs like the liquid they had turned into. She had watched me as I got up to the top. There was a flat part of the roof, just big enough to sit on before you could push yourself down the slope and into the snow. I got there with Lil's voice yelling "Alright Willa! Let her rip!" behind me.

Right.

Everyone below me was not as small as I thought they should be. They should have looked like tiny little ants. I felt like I was high enough up that they should look like ants. I felt like I was high enough that they shouldn't have been visible at all. I squinted my eyes at them to make them seem smaller, to make the reality of the situation match the big fears in my mind.

There was no way I was sliding down those snowy shingles.

So there I was, a woman clinging to a sled, sitting on a roof in a snow storm. A terrified woman sitting on a sled on a roof in a snowstorm. What. In. The. World?

I looked back in my mind at myself in the cozy café and said, "Great job Willa. Look at what thinking has wrought!"

"Wrought huh?" Jacob's voice came pouring in behind me, like heat. Like the heat that was filling me as embarrassment rushed in. "I don't hear that word too often."

"Yes, well, it's a good word." Is all I could muster. I was embarrassed and scared and clinging to the rope on the sled for dear life and I couldn't really think of a better defense for my word choice in that moment.

"Oh, it's a great word. Very powerful. Very dramatic," he said. He was sitting by me now, balanced perfectly on the roof top. He pulled his knees up close to his chest and rested his arms on top of them. "What else you got?"

"What other words?" I asked, confused.

"Yes. What other words would you like to say? They might be your last after all..." he said with a shrug.

"See? You acknowledge that I might die doing this too!" I said.

"Well, you've been sitting up here with that terrified look on your face so long that you've convinced me. This is life and death isn't it?"

"Yes. Life and death. It really, truly is."

"Willa, you will not die on that sled."

"I might," I said defiantly.

"You know what I think? I think you might not live if you don't get on that sled."

"What?" I asked. My lips were starting to freeze in the cold and forming the "w" sound felt funny.

"I think that you've been walking around this place in a daze and you need to wake up and live. This is just the trick."

I looked at him then and it was all too clear to me that he was a therapist and a very good one at that.

"You know I'm right don't you?" he said gently.

I looked down at my gloved hands and simply nodded. Then his hands appeared in front of my eyes as he took the sled from me. He climbed on then patted the space in front of him.

"Get on," he said. His voice was commanding but gentle, like a storm of softly falling snowflakes that somehow takes over the world.

I looked at his kind eyes, his smile that could stop a blizzard and then I climbed on the sled. He was strong and steady behind me, a brace for my weak spine and he wrapped his arms in front of me to grab hold of the rope and to secure me in place. I was vaguely aware of how close we were to each other, how I could feel his breath through my hat, how our gloves were touching, how our boots squeaked when they brushed up against each other on the sled, but I was still too terrified to really think about it. If I had, I might have moved but as it was, I was scared and he was the only balm, the only cure for my fear. The only thing that was getting me off of this roof.

"Ok Willa, are you ready to fly?" he asked.

I closed my eyes and said, "I don't think so but let's just go anyway!"

We slowly lurched forward and down. Down, down, down we went. We were an angle, the edge of a triangle. We were a diagonal line cutting through the air and we were fast. Then, before I knew it, we had reached the edge of the roof and then we were away. Away from any surface, any rules anything solid and we were air. We flew and arched and floated, Jacob and I. I could hear his laughter behind me, a warm and deep and full sound that took up all the room in the sled. Then I heard another sound, one that I hadn't heard often enough lately; my own laughter.

It wasn't as brittle or as hoarse as I had expected. It wasn't like your voice when you wake up in the morning, crackly and out of use. No, it was just my laugh, strong and steady, the way that it was supposed to be and our laughter harmonized, mine and Jacob's. It filled the air with song and I felt like a bird. Flying fast and singing strong.

We landed with a soft thud and then slid along the well-worn path of snow, the trail that had been blazed by those surrounding us with smiles and cheers. They rushed to us as we came to a stop. Lil was clapping and cheering as she ran to me, Drew on her heels ready with a high five.

I was aware of them, of their joy, of their friendship but it all seemed muted like it was in slow motion. Not because it wasn't real or beautiful or full of joy and love, but because it was faded compared to what had happened on that sled.

I had flown. I had laughed. I had soared.

There, on that sled with Jacob, was a universe all unto itself because there, I had lived for the first time in a long time and there, he was. With his arms around me, smiling. We had made that world together, woven it with our laughter and flight and it was vivid and moving in real time. It was where I was living and everything else seemed otherworldly. We were there together and that was more real than anything in that snow covered yard.

* * *

That afternoon, everyone was still there. No one wanted to leave, tucked in as we were against the cold. Like a couple cuddling underneath the covers, we all pulled in close and enjoyed the moment.

Lil set out board games and the makings for sandwiches and we all piled our bread with meat and cheese and the game boards with pieces. The room sounded like friendship and smelled like Chile which Lil had set to simmering on the stove. I watched the snow fall in fat, intricate flakes on the street outside, swirling in circles around street lamps and park benches and I decided that this was goodness itself.

I sat on a bar stool while Lil kept busy behind me at the counter and just watched the scene in front of me. Drew and Jacob had gotten out their guitars and had gone to work on Drew's song. I could see their heads huddled close together as they looked down at each string like it held the magic and mystery of love. I hoped for Drew's sake that it did.

"That boy is too good to be true," Lil said behind me.

I turned to her and saw that she was watching them like I was and she was captivated by the music of her son.

"He's pretty perfect Lil," I said. "I never knew teenage boys came as sweet and as thoughtful and as downright fun as Drew."

"He's always been that way," Lil said with a smile. "Even when he didn't have any reason to be."

I wondered what she meant and then Jacob's prodding to hear their story echoed in my mind. I saw my opportunity and I took it.

"I'm sure he's always had every opportunity to be happy with you as his mother, Lil," I said. I hoped that my statement would lead more as a question, more as an opportunity for her to expand her words and share.

Lil looked at me with fierce love in her eyes.

"I would give anything in the world for my love to be all he's ever needed to be happy. If that was the case, he would never know a sad day in his life. There are things that life throws that are just plain hard though and even a mom can't make it all better sometimes," she said.

My heart lurched at the seriousness of her answer and worry began to creep in on me.

"What do you mean Lil? Is Drew ok?"

"He is now but for a while there he wasn't. When Drew was little, we found out that he had cancer," she said the word like it was poison in her mouth. Like she was spitting it out.

"Oh my goodness!" I said. "When?"

"We found out when he was four. We caught it early but that didn't make the treatments any easier. I'll never forget how absolutely torturous it was to watch him throw up after chemo, to watch his hair, that hair that I combed every morning fall out. For a parent, I think that's as close to hell on earth as you can get."

I looked over at Drew. Smiling, easy going, smart, perfect Drew and my heart lurched at the thought of him laying in a hospital bed.

"I can't even imagine Lil." I finally said.

"Please, don't try!" She told me with a smile and a little shove.

"It's too depressing."

"Well, what happened?" I asked.

"Oh, you know, we just got through it. Mostly thanks to Jake, and this place really. Drew's dad was always in and out of the picture, that is until he got sick and things got hard. Then he was mostly out of the picture. Jake was in school at the time but he moved in with me to help out with everything. He was the best. He went to Doctor's appointments, cooked us dinner, cleaned up puke, let me cry on his shoulder, all of it. I couldn't have done it all without him."

I looked over at Jacob, teaching his nephew to play guitar. The same nephew that he had helped nurse and comfort. I looked from Lil to Jacob and Drew. I was sitting between them all, stuck in the vortex of their love, in a substance that was thick and strong and unrelenting and it filled the room with its presence.

"One day," Lil continued, "a particularly hard day that had put both of us through the ringer mind you, I was driving Drew home from chemo. He was laying down in the back seat, pale as can be and trying not to throw up. We were talking about space. You know, rocket ships and stars and astronauts. That was his favorite thing in the world back then and it could always cheer him up. I would say a planet and he would tell me everything he knew about it. He was so smart even then.

Well, he finally fell asleep which always put me at ease back then. At least when he slept he didn't feel the sickness you know? Anyway, he fell asleep and I kept driving. I didn't know where I was going exactly but I just drove and cried and railed at God in my head. I would have done it out loud but I didn't want to wake up Drew. So there I was, in the middle of my breakdown and I saw it. An old building with a huge turret and chipping paint with a for sale sign on it."

"It was this place wasn't it?" I asked.

"Yep. It sure was. I saw the turret and it immediately reminded me of a rocket ship. I can't really explain it but something just rose up in me. A sense of determination or desperation or something but I had to have it. I had to turn it into a space ship for my Drew. I wanted to do it for him, to give him someplace that he could imagine and thrive and chase his passions. My Dad had died a year before, which is a whole heartbreak in and of itself, and I had some inheritance money from him so I bought it. That same day and then the rest of it just kind of fell into place."

"Drew lit up for the first time in a year when I told him what we were going to do to the place. He loved every minute of the renovations. It gave him so much joy." She glowed as she remembered, stuck on an image of a little boy's smile.

"Anyway, we opened up a week after he went into remission and he's not relapsed since."

I paused for a minute, letting it all sink in.

"So that's why you love each other like you do. You know how to cling for dear life and never let go." I said.

"Exactly, Willa!" she said with a pointed finger. "We have our sad story and the memories still break my heart but that story got us here." She pointed to her heart when she said "here" like the place that their relationship occupied transcended the physical realm. Like they existed in her heart too.

I had tears in my eyes as I smiled at her. Not because I was sad but because her story had stirred something in me. It had shown me that even in the midst of all the sadness that life rains down on us, there was a chance for good to come, for happiness to return.

"Lil, you are a beautiful mother. Thank you for sharing your story with me."

She smiled at me as she reached over and squeezed my hand. "We all have stories, Willa. They're our gifts to give."

I decided that sometime soon, I would return the favor.

Chapter 8

Willa

After a week or so, my days began to settle into a rhythm. I would wake up to the face of the Alien on my dresser greeting me, my first and steady friend like the sunshine or the air. I would get dressed, a depressing task in general because it was simply a reminder that I had no one to dress for. No one to impress or to show off my figure to.

I had worked hard to get that figure, had joined a gym the second that Ollie had proposed so that I could be in perfect wedding dress shape. Quinn had joined with me, making me wear a shirt that said "Sweating for the Wedding".

"I'm joining for moral support." She had said but the second I saw her eyes wander all over every male trainer I called her bluff. We had spent hours at that gym and I had gotten to the place I wanted to be. I liked my toned arms in my strapless wedding dress. I liked my toned legs in my honeymoon bikinis.

Now, it was all covered up under sweaters and jeans in a cold

Colorado winter.

It was just as well. No need to be reminded of the hours I had poured into something that would never be. So, I would slip into my winter wardrobe and head downstairs to get to work on Lil's books.

It was nice to have a rhythm, a routine. It felt good to depend on something and to have some sense of control over my time and energy. It was becoming normal and I found comfort in it.

There was also a rhythm to the café. People would come in and out like sections in a band and I began to recognize them and their sounds and notes and styles.

There was the mom with the newborn that would stop by on her way to the gym to pick up a coffee. I could tell by the wild-eyed look she had and the way that her fingers turned white as she gripped the cup that that coffee was more than a beverage, it was a lifeline for her in her state of newborn sleeplessness and sacrifice and love.

There was the book club that came in on Wednesday evenings, women in their forties who sported a new home made hat created to match the theme of whatever they were reading that week. They would laugh and drink iced tea and their hats would dance around like characters on their head, moving and swaying to the song of their friendship.

There were the families. All of them with children that lit up the place like stars in the sky. For them, Lil always had free cookies and coloring books and compliments galore. They were the jewels in her chest, the treasure that filled the place.

There were the businessmen that held lunch meetings there, marching in with their laptops and lists, closing deals left and right. Lil knew the details of every single one, what they did, what they needed, and it only took her a matter of seconds to start referring me to anyone that needed a CPA. She had sent me off like a snowball rolling through town and before I knew it, I had a nice little business taking off.

Then there was Jacob.

He was there every day without fail, to fill up on coffee, food, and family. I had begun to understand that he was as regular a fixture as the lights or the coffee maker not only in the café's life but in Lil's and Drew's.

Especially because it seemed that Tuesday nights, when he and his band played, everything about the life of the café connected and met in equilibrium, like it was at it's perfect, comfortable place where all was right.

His music gave sound and movement to the soul of the place and I knew that Lil wanted it that way.

I was starting to love every part of this new small town existence until the fact that February had arrived hit me like an arrow. And not a nice arrow like one from Cupid. No, this arrow was more like a sledgehammer that had the power and agility to be shot with quickness and accuracy right at my heart.

I dreaded Valentines Day. Dreaded the inevitable flowers and decorations that Lil would put out, the couples walking hand in hand, the sappiness and love. I didn't begrudge those people that had all of that. They deserved to be happy if they could be. I just didn't want to be reminded that I didn't anymore.

Still, I could not stop time and February came in all of it's red, rosy, annoying splendor. It reminded me of scarlet fever and in my head, I sang "Ring around the rosy, pockets full of posies…".

Each day pulled me closer to Valentine's Day, like I was on some conveyor belt taking me to a trash compactor and that belt was metal and I was a magnet and no matter how hard I tried, I was stuck to it, governed by the laws of nature and science and plain bad luck.

I went to bed on the thirteenth hoping to just plow through

the next day, to simply get it done like an item on a to-do list but sleep evaded me. I couldn't stop thinking about Valentine's Day with Ollie.

We always ate Mexican food. Big steaming plates of Fajitas and deep bowls of salsa. I like the way the skillets full of food sizzle when they set them down, the way the cast iron holds in the heat like a child grabbing a cookie; unrelenting and white hot. I told Ollie that I couldn't think of a better metaphor for love than a table full of fajitas, that love should always sizzle and be white hot even when it was far removed from the initial flame. That it should always satisfy and fill and taste delicious.

When I told him that, with mariachi music playing behind my voice he had laughed at me between bites. He had said, "Alright then, may our love be like fajitas!" Because he always let me see things the way I see them and then celebrated it.

We had clinked our Margaritas together then, toasting to our fajita love but it backfired and sent a grain of salt from the rim of the glass flying into my eye. It stuck in my contact and that tiny little thing felt like a boulder of fire in my eye. Ollie handed me napkin after napkin as I wiped my runny mascara and watery eyes until finally, the rogue grain was free. His eyes were full of concern as he said he was sorry and asked if I was ok and I swore to myself that it was the most romantic moment ever. He and I toasting to fajita love and wiping salt out of my eye. It was us; comfortable yet deep, informal yet special and it became our tradition.

That night in my room at the Inn, I let every detail of those celebrations replay in my mind, every bite, every laugh, every kiss, every smile, I could taste it all yet I longed for it, craved it like a person starving. The tears came like they always did and that's how I fell asleep, with tears flowing down my face onto my pillow, without Ollie there to hand me a napkin to wipe them away.

* * *

I woke up in a daze on the 14th.

I knew what day it was and I planned on simply getting through. After getting ready, I went downstairs, prepared to throw myself at Lil's messy books like a mop on a dirty floor. I pictured myself like a raggedy old mop, wiping myself all over the mess, soaking it up, wearing it, losing myself in it, moving it all around and then dunking myself in the water again, washing it off, cleansing myself only to return to the dirt. That's what I had felt like ever since Ollie had died; like I was an old mop that just kept diving into the mess of hurt on every Holiday or anniversary. I'd skulk around on the floor, on rock bottom and then lift myself up to the bucket, up to the place where I would cleanse myself of it all, find a place of ok-ness only to be thrown right back at the stain and dirt and mess of my heart on the next Holiday. It was a cycle I felt doomed to repeat.

Like a mop.

I assumed that the Café would be decked out in Cupid cutouts and hearts so I thought that the best thing to do would be to look at my feet while I walked right to the office. Lil would undoubtedly come find me in a few minutes and bring some coffee and food with her.

I rounded the corner at the bottom of the staircase ready to brace myself against the festivity but what I found wasn't nearly as assaulting as I had thought. Lil had opted out of the tacky heart shaped everything and had decided on simple bouquets of roses and white twinkle lights all around the room. There were red and white buds standing guard like sentries at every table and the stage and ceiling had been strung with extra lights.

The effect was more of a nod to Valentines Day instead of a whole production of it. Like the Holiday was simply making a cameo because the café and the life therein, they were the main characters. Relief washed over me and it must have shown on my face.

"You look like you just got the best news of your life!" Lil said.

"Oh, I just love your Valentine's Day decorations. Not too much. I appreciate it." I said.

"Less is more don't you think?" Lil asked as she gave me a sideways hug punctuated with a squeeze of my shoulders.

I wanted to laugh a little to myself because Lil was not a "less is more" kind of person in most respects but something told me not to point it out. Lil was a single mother after all. Maybe her feelings about Valentine's Day were in the same dreary boat as mine.

"Well, I say 'well done Madame,'" I said as I pantomimed taking my hat off to her.

We made our way to the counter, while I thanked Lil silently for creating an atmosphere that wasn't too much like rubbing alcohol for my injured soul, that I could actually sit in and enjoy. I thanked her again, out loud this time as she brought me a plate of strawberry crepes with homemade whipped cream.

"It's a good thing I don't have anyone to impress tonight because with food like this, I'm going to put on some Holiday weight but it'll be year round! You spoil me, Lil!" I said with a smile.

"Oh Willa, you have already impressed plenty of people around here."

"Oh yeah? Who?" I asked with sarcasm in my tone.

Before Lil could answer, Jacob walked in the door with Drew following behind him. Actually, Drew's torso and legs followed behind him but his head was lost behind a giant bouquet of Lilies.

The smell of the flowers reached us before Drew and Jacob, pulling a smile from Lil like a bee pulls pollen out of a flower.

"I wonder who those are for?" Lil said with a teasing smile as she put her index finger up to her mouth.

"You know they're for you, Mom," Drew said. "Here you go.

Lilies for Lil. Happy Valentines Day! Love you!" He handed them to her and then pulled her in for a hug. She reached up and put one hand on his cheek while she kissed the other.

It was sweet in all the ways that something could be sweet and I decided that this was the moment I would associate with Valentine's Day this year.

"Well, that was just perfection, Drew!" I said.

"Ahh, it's no big deal. I do it every year," he said with a shrug. "Uncle Jake has helped me with it since I was a kid."

I looked over at Jacob who was looking down at his fingernails like he was embarrassed by getting caught.

"Does he now?" I asked with a smile. "Well aren't you two just the best brother and son around! Lil, I think they've earned some Crepes!"

"They certainly have! Sit! Sit!" she said as she shuffled them over to a bar stool on either side of me. A plate was in front of them before they even got their coats off.

Jacob scooted in beside me and our shoulders brushed. It seemed natural enough but as soon as it happened, I felt him stiffen a little. He sat up straighter and mumbled "Sorry Willa."

"It's ok Jacob. Shoulders touch sometimes. It's nothing monumental." I said. I had meant it to sound like a joke, a comment to put him at ease but he must have thought I was being snarky. I do that sometimes; mismatch my words and my tone. I wish I could be one of those people that could master both but I'm just not.

"No, it isn't monumental. It doesn't matter to me if it doesn't matter to you," he said as he cleared his voice.

I smiled at him to try and ease the tension and he held my gaze, smiling back for a minute. Then his smile kind of fell away slowly and he just stared at me for a few seconds longer. I didn't know whether I should look away or just keep holding that moment there, like a hammock hanging between our eyes. Something was happening, though. In his eyes…

"Happy Valentine's Day, Willa," Jacob said quietly. Actually, he said it almost tenderly. It was quiet and gentle like he really, truly meant it. Like there was nowhere else he would rather be than eating strawberry crepes with me on Valentines Day and I didn't know what to make of it.

I waited for a millisecond to decipher how my heart was responding, I knew it wasn't deaf, that it had picked up on his tone and I expected it to send up signs of panic, of revulsion because this man was not Ollie but it didn't. It had sped up a little bit in response to his tone, his smile, his eyes but it wasn't panic. It was the same feeling I had had with him when we had flown off of the roof. In that instance, I had attributed my reaction to the exhilaration of what we had done together. I had put it from my mind, not ready to deal with it. But now, here it was again. Was it… pleasure? I didn't know. I couldn't know. I couldn't go there today of all days.

"Happy Valentine's Day, Jacob," I said quickly in my most dismissive and authoritative voice possible. Maybe a little too quickly because he looked down at his plate suddenly, like he had been scolded. I felt bad because that was not what I meant to do. Again. Actually, I felt a little sad too because I liked him looking at me and he had stopped too soon. The realization of all of these thoughts was too much for me but my heart was still racing a little bit and now my head was panicking a little bit too because I was afraid I had hurt his feelings.

What a mess I was.

I took a gigantic gulp of coffee hoping to drown everything inside of me in caffeine and darkness.

"So, do either of you have any plans for tonight? Drew, are you taking Sophie anywhere?" I asked, trying to appear casual instead of the frantic mess that I was inside.

"Nah, not yet," Drew said sheepishly. "I'm putting all of my eggs in the song to ask her to prom. I don't think I'm brave enough to ask her out yet."

"Don't be silly Drew! She would be lucky to have you for her Valentine! I'm sure every girl at that school would feel lucky to have you as their Valentine."

"Well, he's mine all mine!" Lil yelled from the other end of the counter.

"Ok, Mom," Drew said through a bite of crepes.

"What about you Jacob?" I asked tentatively. I was trying to change the subject and break the tension from earlier. Who knew if it would work.

"I'll just be here, playing like every other Tuesday," he said with a small, sad smile. Was there somewhere else he wanted to be? Someone else he wanted to be with? Why did I care?

I had forgotten all about the fact that Valentine's Day had fallen on the night that he played, and to my complete and utter surprise again, my heart was excited at the prospect. I didn't know what was going on! I had fallen asleep last night aching for what I had had with Ollie, for fajita-love and him but now, here I was, looking forward to Jacob serenading me (and the rest of the room) on Valentine's Day.

I took another big, long, giant, gulp of coffee because, well, it was too early for something stronger.

"Will you be here?" Jacob asked me. The soft, tender tone had returned. I could hear hope in his words. Maybe my turning the subject had helped.

Would I? I didn't have anything else to do but what if the sad thoughts came back. I didn't want to risk running out of here in tears in the middle of his show again. That was humiliating enough the first time. I also didn't want to be all alone in my room tonight though either. Then there was the actual, real, desire I had to be here, to hear him sing, and see him smile, and oh my word, what was happening to me?

"Umm, well, Valentine's Day isn't really my thing anymore. I don't know, maybe." Was all I managed. I punctuated my attempts at nonchalance and general free-spiritedness with a shrug and another sip of coffee, this one was smaller and more ladylike, but I looked at Jacob out of the corner of my eye.

He was smiling and looking down at his plate. Why was he smiling? Did he see right through me? Did he know that my mind and heart were the epitome of female mood swings right now? He was a shrink after all, he probably knew.

"Well, if you come, I'll try not to make you cry ok? Only happy songs, I promise," he said.

"Jacob, in my experience, it's the happy love songs that make the lonely people the saddest on Valentine's Day," I said.

"Are you lonely, Willa?" He asked.

There was that look again, the same one he gave me on the day that we met, the same one he had given me on the roof and the sled. It was quiet and interested and concerned with not a trace of humor or ease. It was fierce and utterly interested. It was the way a neurosurgeon would look in the middle of brain surgery. It made me feel like he wanted to know the answer more than anything in the world. Like he wanted to know and then he wanted to fix it. It was disarming and comforting and made my heart speed up yet again.

"Yes," I said in a whisper. It came out before I could stop it.

"Someday Willa, I'd like to know why. When you're ready to tell me, that is. Tonight, though, just come and have a little fun. I know better than anyone that there's nothing better to cure loneliness than music, Lil and Drew, and Lil's cooking." He ended with a smile, took one last bite, and then got up to leave.

As he was telling Drew goodbye, I watched him and wondered how he knew about loneliness. I wondered what his story was, where he had been, and I wondered at my desire to want to know all of it in the first place. Then I thought about how he had asked, in a roundabout way, to hear mine and I wondered if I would tell him.

Did he really want to know my baggage? To look at the battered, big, trunks of hurt and anger and confusion that I had been carrying around for the last year and a half? Did he really want to take that in, to pick it up and test the weight of it? Because, the second that someone shares their story with you, it becomes part of what you carry around, part of your load. That's what he was asking for and I think he meant it. I knew he did because I knew that I felt the same way.

* * *

I finished my breakfast and went into the office to work on Lil's books but I couldn't focus. The numbers snaked around on the page, the words swirled and danced and jumbled. Despite the plan to escape here, to forget about the emotions I had woken up with, not to mention the others that had made their debut at breakfast, I couldn't focus. It seemed that my heart would not be ignored today.

I had to do something to clear my head so I decided to take a little walk. The weather had been unseasonably warm the last week and, even though it was the middle of February, people were out and about in short sleeves and sandals.

Nothing about this place was what I had expected.

I walked aimlessly, enjoying the sun on my skin. It felt so good like the world was throwing a blanket around me, hemming me in with light and warmth and fresh air. The sky was a giant ceiling of uninterrupted blue, a long run-on sentence full of promises of spring. A cloud could have stopped it, like a period at the end of a sentence but none could be found so it rambled on and on, waxing poetic of all things beautiful and boundless.

I walked underneath it, passing through its presence, taking it all in. I let it refresh me and inspire me. The way that it was saturated with blue, so bright and clean and full of itself was amazing. It could be this, fully and completely *this*; blue and warm and spring-like even in the middle of winter. It wasn't supposed to be. It was supposed to be cold and frozen and white, devoid of color and hope. It shouldn't look like this; it shouldn't have surrendered to the sun.

But it had.

Even in the midst of winter, when all things are frozen and lifeless, two weeks after a blizzard, this day was here.

I walked for block after block, trying to come to terms with where my heart was at. I still loved Ollie, still ached for him but now, I could sense a stirring towards Jacob. I couldn't ignore the way that my heart had raced at his voice and interest, the way that I was looking forward to seeing him, to hearing him tonight, and I couldn't ignore that he was handsome in an irrefutable, laws of nature and female attraction kind of way.

Maybe nothing would come of it. Maybe, he wasn't even interested in me. But maybe he was. I looked up at the sun-drenched, bright blue, winter sky and saw Jacob. I had been in winter for years, living in a frigid January for a long, long time, but here was this day; this sunny bright, warm February Day.

I wasn't completely fooled. I knew that it was still technically winter and that the sadness and grief might sneak back in like a blizzard at some point, but outside with the sun on my skin and warmth all around me, with people sporting their summer clothes and kids blowing bubbles in the park across the street, I decided to give in.

I decided that I would go tonight, that I would enjoy the sunshine in my winter.

I walked back to the café carried along by the unfamiliar push of happiness. It led me onward, towards the place that had become my new world. As I approached the café, I smiled at the sight of the rocket ship. It climbed up the side of the building, pulling everything upwards and towards the sun. I remembered all that it symbolized for Lil and Drew and how it had, in a way taken them away from earth and their troubles towards new and good things. I knew it was dramatic but I felt like somehow, I was riding the coattails of that ascent and beginning to make it mine. I felt like I had been soaring upwards ever since I arrived here but a part of me hoped that I wouldn't fall or get burned by the jet stream.

"Slow and steady, Willa," I told myself.

I walked up the front porch and opened the door, my state of self-reflection and pep-talkery still fresh in my mind when I saw her. There standing at the counter laughing with Lil was my sister, Quinn.

Chapter 9

Jacob

I hadn't meant to say it the way that I had. I knew that the words had come out sounding too romantic, too interested. I guess I shouldn't have been surprised. Deep down, I wanted to say those words to her in a romantic context. I would have loved to have been able to wish her a Happy Valentine's Day but for real. Over dinner with candles and flowers and all the other stuff.

I had almost risked making that happen. I had almost bought her some flowers when I went with Drew to buy Lil's. The feel of her in front of me, tucked close on that sled, of her hair flowing back into my face and waving its strawberry scent under my nostrils fueled me. I had the bouquet picked out in my mind, roses and daffodils, had almost reached for my wallet but then I second guessed myself. Something stopped me and I'm glad it had.

Despite my own self-censorship at the flower shop, all those thoughts were still running through my mind when I saw her at the café. I was still thinking about her laughter and the way we had shared a moment (it had to have been a moment!) on the sled, the way we had flown together. It was all still there and I couldn't help myself.

"Happy Valentine's Day, Willa." I had said.

In a sappy, meaningful, almost longing tone and it was even off-putting to me. I might as well have bought her ten dozen roses. I might as well have professed my undying love for her. I might as well have told her I wanted her to have my children, twelve sons to be exact and all of them would be allowed to play football in the house every second of every day.

At least that's what her face made it seem like.

She seemed so shocked, so embarrassed, so put off and it was more than a little bit deflating.

I hadn't meant to let her know that I was interested. I still knew so little about her, and it seemed like there was a lot to know. Sure, I knew that I had developed feelings for her but I wasn't quite ready for *her* to know yet.

Now I didn't know if I ever wanted her to know. Or, really, if she ever wanted to know.

I walked to my office, while I inflicted mental self-flagellation upon myself. Why did I do this? Hadn't I learned my lesson with Jenny?

The signs had all been there with her, the reserve, the tepid kisses. Jenny never lit up near me or matched the level of my feelings.

I remembered how on our first Christmas together, I had arranged for a carriage ride through her favorite park. We round around the paths, tucked under a blanket and I grabbed her hand and held it tight. We stopped at a little Pavilion where I had set up hot chocolate and cookies for us and had a few of my college buddies playing Christmas carols. I asked her to dance and we did. I gave her a pearl necklace and she put it on. I poured her hot chocolate and she drank it. And so it went. She played her part as I directed the show.

"This is so nice Jake, so romantic!" She had said. "I didn't know we were at this point yet, though. I don't have anything for you." She had the decency to look down when she said that but then, like a perfectly timed distraction, she looked up at me with soulful, puppy-dog eyes like she knew she could do no wrong.

We had been dating for ten months, ten months that had been filled with Drew's illness right on the coattails of my father's death and I had told her I loved her. I had clung to her really and saw her as the cure to all of my ills. While my world was crumbling and falling to the ground like a hot air balloon with its flame turned off, she had been standing there and I had grabbed on for dear life. I thought that called for some Christmas magic and romance but she hadn't. My heart sunk a little but I put on a happy face.

"You don't need to give me anything, Jenny. I love you." I said as I pulled her to me.

"Yeah, you too." She had said. I could still hear her voice. It sounded pinched and distracted.

If I had been paying any attention, if I had looked around at my world and the people that were in it, away from my problems and my need to cling to somebody or something, I would have seen it. I would have seen who she was looking at while I told her I loved her.

The thought bolstered me. I remembered how bad she had hurt me and how deeply she had betrayed me and it solidified all that regret from this morning.

I knew that look on Willa's face. It was the same as Jenny's. It was a look full of polite reserve and discomfort. Like they were being prevailed upon to endure the affections of a horrid man like me and I didn't want to deal with that again. I couldn't.

My heart had no desire to be broken and that's what it seemed like Willa would lead to. A gigantic shattering of an already glued back together piece of me.

* * *

I powered through the morning, armed with Lil's coffee and plenty of appointments. Angie fed me patient after patient like quarters in an arcade game and their problems became my cure. I dove head first into listening to each and every one, letting their words and feelings and angst and hope pour over me like a waterfall. A waterfall that washed me clean of my memories of Jenny and my Dad and my feelings for Willa, for the moment anyway.

The submersion in my work was helpful. I love what I do, genuinely love it, and I think that there's a deep and lasting healing that comes from talking to someone and listening. I couldn't help but feel a string of thought pulling at the back of my mind, though. Its tug pulled and redirected my thoughts inward, pointing like a cross-stitched arrow down to my own self.

How often had I done this? How often had I thrown myself into this job or my music or both simultaneously to escape? How often had I decided to listen to and try to fix other people's emotional problems instead of dealing with my own?

If I was being honest, I had done it a lot.

I knew that I should enjoy self-reflection and self-awareness. It was what I pushed my patients to do all of the time but, honestly, I didn't. If I wanted to be a patient, I'd go see someone.

Between patients, I leaned back in my desk chair and rubbed my hands over my face. I scratched my beard absentmindedly, trying to get rid of an itch just underneath it. I got up and walked over to my window which looked out over the park across the street.

The day was warm and beautiful and people, couples mostly, walked hand in hand through the park. It was a pretty scene but

I wasn't touched by it. It was the same park that I had taken Jenny to that Christmas, and after years of on again off again, it was the same park that I had proposed to her in five years ago.

As if by instinct, I looked towards the western corner of the expansive lawn, the one where the path wound into a copse of trees that glowed like flames in the fall. They were barren now but still they were there, marking the spot where Jenny had said no. She had said more than no actually. She had said words that cut deeper than that, words that sliced and seared and destroyed.

She hadn't just said no. She had told me why she was saying no. Why she would never marry me but that she would marry my college roommate, and very soon.

I closed my eyes and pictured myself kneeling down on one knee, ring extended like an offering to the goddess that I thought she was and my stomach turned in disgust.

It was all so ridiculous really. The fact that I was so hurt by her, that it was still affecting me years later was stupid. I was acting like some dramatic love sick teenager. Like the girl who was crying on my couch yesterday because she had convinced herself that she was emotionally damaged because the guy she had kissed at some party wasn't calling her back.

I had moved on, made a life for myself without her and it was a good one. I was ok. More than ok really and I had firmly decided a long time ago that I was fine being a bachelor but then Willa had come to town and had taken my heart on a ride. I had allowed myself to hope but it had been fragile. Fragile enough to fall to pieces based on one look from her. I exhaled in frustration, trying to blow out the memories like birthday candles, as I opened my eyes.

I should have waited a few more seconds before doing that though because, there, walking through the park, through the trees, through the places that were scars, was Willa. She walked with perfect posture, her shoulders pulled back tight and her head held high. She looked like a moving sculpture. She was art. Her hair fell gracefully down her back, like a cascade of brown, like chocolate flowing out of a fountain and it begged for me to dip my fingers underneath and enjoy the deliciousness. I watched her walking towards me for a moment before the path wound around and changed directions. I watched her move and smile and mesmerize me.

What was I thinking?!

This day had gotten away from me, that was certain. I pulled hard on the chord of the blinds shutting her and Jenny and the beauty and sunlight out.

* * *

"Drew's here!" Angie called to me. It was a useless announcement really because I had heard him arrive. His laughter and teasing snaked under my door before Angie told me.

He let himself into my office with his ever-present smile on tight.

"Hey, Uncle Jake!"

"Hey, Bud!" I said.

"Are we still on for my lesson today? I assumed we were but then on my way over here, I wondered if I maybe should have called first. You know, since it's Valentine's Day and whatever."

"You never need to call Drew. You're always welcome here and yes, we're still on." I said with a sigh. I knew I should have tried to be a little more upbeat but the day was weighing on me and I just couldn't.

"Are you ok?" he asked. The boy had the same keen emotional perception as his mom and I hated and loved it all at the same time.

"Yeah, I'm fine. Just a long day. Forget about it. Let's just dive right in."

He watched me as I grabbed two guitars off of the wall and handed my Dad's to him. I could see the wheels turning in his mind, the memories that he knew I had been replaying today, the feelings that he assumed I was having.

"Hey Uncle Jake, what are you going to play tonight?" He asked me. I didn't know why he wanted to know but I answered him anyway.

"Just a handful of classic love songs that most people will know. It's just filler really."

"Nah, I doubt it."

"Why do you want to know?"

"You have great taste in music. Especially romantic music. Just trying to learn as much as I can from you," he said with a teasing smile.

"Drew, you know my history with women. You know how things worked out with Jen. You might be better off ignoring my tastes." I said as I tuned my guitar.

"Uncle Jake, I do know your history with Jenny and none of it had anything to do with you. She was crazy, end of story. Mom never liked her you know?"

I stopped fiddling with the guitar and looked up at Drew with mild surprise. "She didn't? She was always friendly to her when I was around."

"Well sure when you were around but as soon as you guys left, mom would just go to town, listing all the stuff that she hated about her." Drew popped a piece of gum in his mouth as he talked. He offered me a piece and I took it.

The peppermint exploded in my mouth as I asked, "What kind of stuff would she say?"

"Oh, all kinds of stuff. She wore too much makeup, she had a fake looking smile, she was too stuck up, she wasn't nice enough to you, her shoes were too showy. She was self-centered. She said her 'r's' weird. Really, it was something different every time but she would always end her tirade by saying 'Drew, don't you ever force me to put up with a woman like that. You choose wisely son, because if you don't, I will have to choose between being my normal amazing self and one of those terrible mom's who can't get along with her daughter in law. Don't make me the bad guy!"

I laughed out loud because I could hear Lil saying every single word that Drew had just recited. I could see her red hair dancing around like a bonfire as she spat out every word and feeling. She was right too. Jenny was all of those things.

"Well Drew, all I can say is, your mom was right. I wish she would have told me all of those things too. It would have saved me a lot of heartache."

"She was just trying to be supportive and whatever you know? Cause of all the stuff you've always done for us."

"Yeah, I get that but still, I would have listened to her. You two are all I've got and I'd take you over a woman like Jenny any day."

"Anyone would take us over her! We're awesome and she's a jerk!"

I laughed again because he was right.

"Yeah, she is."

"She really is Uncle Jake. Really! A total, complete jerk! I hope you know that. I hope you know that all that stuff that happened wasn't because there was anything wrong with you or you didn't love her well. It was her Uncle Jake. All her." He looked at me intensely. All humor was gone from his face and I was taken aback for two reasons.

Number one being that what he said was powerful. It hit me like water in a swimming pool on a hot day. It cooled and comforted and refreshed me because it was good to hear from someone else that what had happened was, by all accounts, wrong. It was something only a jerk would do.

The second reason I was taken aback was because, there in front of me, my nephew had asserted a very powerful and strong opinion. One that wasn't self-centered and immature but that had every trace of respect and value and nuance that words like that need to have. He had said just enough to move me, to get his point across, to help and he had said it because he picked up on my mood and feelings and he cared.

It was completely grown up. He was grown up.

"Drew," I finally said. "Thank you. I'm so unbelievably proud of you."

He looked down as he blushed ever so slightly and then he looked up and said, "Uncle Jake, I'm proud of you because I think you're getting past all that."

"You think so?" I asked with a short laugh. If only he knew what had been running through my head all day.

"Well, are you going to play love songs tonight at the café? Are you going to teach me how to play a love song?" He asked.

"Yeah," I said.

"Then you're getting past it."

I thought about his words, his optimism, and intuitiveness. Maybe there was a trace of truth to what he said but part of me knew it wasn't completely factual. I knew that I still harbored resentment for what had happened. Towards Jenny for her deception and lack of love but also towards myself for clinging to her and turning towards her as a source of joy after my Dad had died. I had self-medicated with her, had depended on her for healing and that's never ok. I couldn't think of how I wouldn't always harbor resentment. I also knew that I still had more than a little bit of reservation about moving forward with pursuing Willa. What if I was just doing the same thing with her, seeking out a relationship for all the wrong reasons. Could I trust myself?

Things were far more complicated than Drew made them out

to be.

I knew I wasn't past it but maybe I was a better actor than I thought. That knowledge gave me hope and stamina for the night that lay ahead- the one that promised to surround me with romance and the woman that seemed to want to share it with me as much as she did the bubonic plague.

Chapter 10

Willa

Quinn and I sat on my bed, surrounded by chocolate wrappers and all of the moments we had missed in each other's lives over the last weeks. We handed each of them over to the other like the sweet gift that they were and we unwrapped every detail like candy.

"Where did you get this chocolate from?" I asked her. "Or should I say, who did you get this from?" I wagged my eyebrows at her, waiting to see if she had any response.

"I got them from a man in a chocolate shop at the airport. He was tall, dark, and about 80 years old and he happily gave them to me as a romantic gesture after I paid him $9.99."

"Well, what a prince!" I said as we laughed.

"I couldn't come see you on this day of all days without chocolate, Wills!"

We devoured the stories each had to share while we ate. Quinn told me about the bad haircut she got a month ago, how the girl was fresh out of beauty school and looked like she was so nervous that she was about to cry with every snip.

"It was all I could do not yell 'Boo!' at her when she turned my chair around to face her. I thought better of it, though. She was jumpy already and she had scissors in her hand so you do the math. Still, it would have been funny. That is until I saw my hair. Atrocious does not do it justice. I swear the left side was three inches longer than the right. I came back the next day and had someone else fix it. I'm assuming the first girl was breathing into a paper bag somewhere in the back..." and on and on her stories went.

Work was good. All of our family was good. She was casually seeing some guy named Chet who was a realtor.

"Why aren't you with 'Chet the realtor' for Valentine's Day then?" I asked with a shove and a smile.

"Come on Wills, you know."

"I know what?"

"You know that no matter who I am seeing, I could not, under any circumstances, let you be alone on Valentine's Day."

She squeezed my hand after she said it, pressing her words into my palm like a note or a promise.

I smiled a small, knowing smile and looked down at my lap. I did know. I knew the minute that I saw her that that was why she was here and I loved her more because of it. We each ate another chocolate in comfortable silence.

"I stopped by the gallery a few weeks ago. It looks good. They still have a few of Ollie's pictures up for sale but most of them were snatched up ages ago," she said cautiously as she gave me a sidelong glance.

"That's good," I said. "Ollie would be happy that it's still up and running." I meant it. He would be, and the fact that my heart didn't plunge to the ground at the mention of him or his work didn't escape me.

Quinn looked at me gauging my reaction. When she saw that her hedging of the subject didn't incite tears or hysterics or a frantic run on the rest of the chocolates, she nodded slowly and got off of the bed. She wandered around the room smiling at the quirky decorations Lil had scattered around until her eyes landed on something tucked below the alien on the dresser. It was the life insurance check I had from Ollie.

"You still haven't deposited this, Wills?" She asked in surprise.

"Not yet," I said sheepishly as I got up and snatched it from her hands.

"You can't just leave a check for that much money sitting around somewhere! You need to deposit it! Do something with it!"

"I know, I will. I just don't know what yet. I want to do something meaningful with it." I said looking down.

"Well think of something and soon!" she said with her eyebrows raised.

She walked back over to the bed to grab another chocolate and I followed.

"So how are you, Wills?" It was one of those "how are you's" with sincerity and understanding behind it. I couldn't just give her a generic "good." She was my sister. I had to get into it.

"Honestly?" I said. "I really, truly don't even know!"

"What do you mean?" Quinn asked through a mouthful of chocolate.

"Well, I've been dreading today like the plague. I cried myself to sleep last night because I was dreading it so badly but then, I woke up this morning, and it's not been nearly as awful as I expected."

"Cause I'm here?" Quinn asked with a wink.

"Partly. But, I don't know, there's more to it."

I paused for a second, debating over what to say, how much to say but then I realized that it was all so confusing and such a mess to me that the only thing I could say was everything because then, I might be able to make sense of it all. Like if I threw the words at Quinn, she could help me put the scrambled mess into an order that actually spelled out a coherent thought or feeling.

"Ok, here's the thing. I don't know what's going on with me, Quinn! I don't understand how I feel or what I'm thinking. I think I need medication really because my head and my heart are like fun house mirrors. Like I can't figure myself out because everything I see is distorted and weird and not what I expected or what I saw the last time I looked at myself."

"Wills, you're not making any sense," she said with a laugh.

"I know! I'm not making *any* sense!" I said as I threw my hands in the air.

"Ok, well then just tell me everything you're feeling and thinking today and we'll figure it out."

"Well, when I woke up, I felt terribly and woefully sad."

Quinn laughed like she always does at my word choice. "Oh, Wills how I've missed your words! Ok, so you were sad. Woefully sad! That's not out of the ordinary, though. You've been sad for a long time. Too long if you ask me."

"Ok, well I didn't ask you, thank you very much!"

"I'm your sister, there's an all time 'ask' thrown out there. So then what."

"Ok, well, then the day progressed. I talked to some of the people I've gotten to know here and something…happened." I said slowly.

"What?"

"Well, one of the people that I've become friends with is Lil's brother, Jacob."

"And the plot thickens!" Quinn said as she clapped her hands together.

"So Jacob and I have had a handful of interactions that have left me feeling, umm, well, *feelings* if you know what I mean and I just realized that that's what they were this morning. The morning after I cried myself to sleep because I missed Ollie so much. What do I do with that Quinn?" My confusion and desperation mixed together creating a kind of helium effect on my voice. It got more high-pitched the longer I talked.

"I'll tell you what you do with that. First of all, you let whatever your heart is saying and doing be. You let it tell you because it knows when all of this, all the sadness and running and hiding is over. It knows when it needs to come out and live again, Wills. Second of all, you're going to tell me every single detail about these 'interactions' you two have had together," she said interaction with air quotes and an eye roll. "Only you would describe it like that, Wills."

I told her everything. I told her how I was crying the first time I saw him and he was singing. I told her about our embarrassing first conversation, the flying, the moments afterwards, the "Happy Valentine's Day". I told her about the way he looks when he talks and the way I feel when I hear his voice. Every detail was splayed out for her so that I could finally make sense of it all.

"Oh Wills, this is good." She finally said.

"Why is it good?" I said almost incredulously.

"Because, you're coming back to us," she said with conviction and joy and tears in her eyes.

"I'm not moving back to Texas, Quinn."

"Oh, I know that! That's not what I mean. I mean, you're starting to live again."

"But how can I? How can I be interested in someone other than Ollie? He's who I chose."

"Yes, you did. You chose him and you guys were so good together, Wills! I'd give anything to change what happened, to be sitting here talking about how your honeymoon went or your plans for kids but that's not how life turned out. What happened is unimaginably awful but now there's this. This chance for you to feel happiness and hope and Wills, you have to take it! I don't care if anything happens with you and Jacob or not. Just, let yourself feel again. That's all I'm asking." She was squeezing my shoulders with both hands at this point and I could see her plea in her eyes, hear it in her voice and feel it in both of our hearts.

"I want to Quinn, I really, truly do. I'm just so conflicted about all of it."

"Wills, Ollie would want you to."

"Maybe he would but I don't know what it's like to even be interested in another man. I don't know what I'll be like, who I'll be without him."

"Well, maybe it's time we find out."

* * *

Two hours later we were sitting downstairs at a table right in front of the stage. Lil had insisted that we sit with her and Drew and she also insisted that she always had to sit front and center. So, there we were with an up close and personal view of Jacob and his band setting up. He had yet to acknowledge my presence and I didn't blame him after the cool reception I had given him at breakfast. Actually, it seemed like he was going out of his way to look in every other direction but my own.

I tried to follow his lead. I tried not to watch him get everything in place, tried not to notice the way his shirt sleeves grew tight around his biceps when he lifted amps and instruments. Quinn did no such thing, though.

"Well, I can see what you see in him, Wills. That's for darn sure!" she said with big eyes.

"Stop it, Quinn!" I whispered as I slapped her arm. "I don't need to be any more embarrassed than I already am around him."

"What do you mean? What do you have to be embarrassed about?"

"Well, every time I'm around him, I do something dramatic or stupid or something."

"Willa, you are always doing dramatic things. That's just who you are so I don't know why you're embarrassed by that and as far as stupid goes? Well, that's just further evidence that you might be developing feelings for him."

"For who?" Lil asked. She had snuck up on us like a ninja but instead of wielding nun chucks, she had steaming hot plates of Fettuccini Alfredo in her hands, like weapons that eradicate hunger.

"Hmm? Oh nobody!" I said as I blushed ten shades of red. I was probably the most festive decoration in the place.

Lil looked at me, saw my reaction and then thought better of pursuing her line of questioning.

"Well, here you go ladies. I'm going to go ahead and set my plate down too and catch a quick bite with you. Drew is running a little late, finishing up his homework so I told Jake to take his place. Hope you don't mind."

"We sure don't!" Quinn said with a gigantic smile.

Lil went and got Jacob to tell him that his food was ready and he followed her to the table. Much too reluctantly I might add.

He said his hellos with little to no enthusiasm and my heart sank a little bit. I couldn't quite tell what his reserve was stemming from. He didn't seem angry at me. He didn't even seem hurt, just kind of separate. His voice and face lacked the friendly ease it usually had. His eyes didn't seem as opened and perceptive to what was going on. It was like he had put sunglasses on and was choosing not to look and see.

"Jacob, this is my sister Quinn. She came for a surprise visit." I said trying to break the ice a little bit.

"Nice to meet you, Quinn. I'm sure that Willa is glad to have you here." Is all he said. His smile was polite but closed off and it was very unlike him. He was like a church with its doors locked and its window shades down. He was usually so open and caring and curious and accepting but tonight, he was shut up tight.

We all fell into an awkward silence then, twisting our noodles around our forks and avoiding eye contact. Jacob was usually so open and friendly, quick to ask questions and get to know new people. It was just one more reason why I knew that he must be superb at his job. Tonight though, he wasn't biting. I looked over and saw Lil studying him with a scowl.

"Jake, what's gotten into you tonight? Where's your smile?" Lil asked with a slight shove. She wasn't all playfulness, though. I could see the concern in her eyes.

"Nothing Lil. I'm fine. I'm actually not very hungry, though. Do you mind if I just get back to setting up?" He asked.

"I don't think you've ever said that to me before. Now I'm really, truly worried!"

"No need to worry sis. Just box it up for me and I'll eat it later," he said and before Lil could answer, he had stood up and turned back towards the stage, turned away from me.

My heart, my fragile, silly, dramatic heart sank a little deeper.

He was obviously not interested in me. I had misread his signals, misread the interest in his eyes, the tenderness in his voice because he wanted nothing to do with me. Absolutely, positively nothing.

How could I have been so silly? How could I have let myself think that I could find happiness with a man that wasn't Oliver? He had been it. My only chance at love and now he was gone forever.

I looked at Jacob with his back to me and then I looked down at my naked ring finger. I was alone and always would be. That was that. Case closed, no need for further review. I, Willa Rose Dunham would never, ever, find love again.

I didn't really know what did me in completely. It could have been the fact that I was again, remembering Ollie and his love, it could have been the happy couples all around us, or it could have been Jacob and the door he had slammed on any conversation or more tonight. Whatever it was, tears were beginning to pool in my eyes.

I felt like a basement that was being flooded. Like there were cracks and problems in my very foundation and no matter how hard I tried, I could not keep the water and sadness from flooding me.

Was I this fragile?

Yes. I decided that I was.

Before I could stop myself, I mumbled some excuse about needing to use the restroom and I made my retreat.

I fumbled through the dining room of the café towards the bathroom but then thought twice about that. I didn't want anyone else running into me in there. I knew myself well enough to know that I was about to have a nice long cry and I didn't want to replay scenes from seventh grade where I huddled in a bathroom stall and cried while other girls talked and put on lip gloss on the other side of my door.

I thought about seventh grade and a fresh wave of self-pity washed over me. I should have known, even back then that this is how I was going to end up. Actually, there was probably some direct correlation between seventh-grade girls that cried in the bathroom at school and thirty-year-old women that cried on Valentine's Day. My whole life read like a graph, a steady sloping line pointing to pathetic. No outliers, no happy little points where I wasn't ridiculous, just this. Emotional drama and loneliness.

I let myself think those things because in the moment, I was in that kind of mood and it felt good to feed the tears with self-pity, it was the kindling to my fire and it was raging now.

Aimlessly, I wandered towards Lil office and I realized why when I saw the door a few feet in front of me. Behind that closed door, there were numbers and papers and pens and a computer. There were problems that only I could solve and there were all the tools that I needed to do it.

Suddenly, a desperate need to throw the door open wide and to launch myself into it overcame me. I needed to be at that desk, working because there, with all of the books and business problems in front of me, I had a purpose. I had a task and I was prepared to do it.

I needed to work because I needed to feel good about myself for a minute. I needed to feel like I had some form of usefulness to lend to another human. Sure, it wasn't love and adoration like I had given to Ollie, like I had thought for a minute that I could give to Jacob, but it was something. Something that was all mine and mine to give.

I pushed open the office door and slowly sat down at the desk. I breathed in a long, slow, steadying breath letting the room and all that it held fill me. I briefly thought about how this moment would be much more powerful and poetic if there were old books somewhere in there. Old books have such a beautiful smell, like all that has ever happened in the world around them and the worlds within them and the loving hands of generation after generation poured themselves out together to make a perfume that saturates and entices the mind and soul. They lend a certain weight and significance to a moment. There weren't any though and I didn't want to waste any time missing them.

This moment, this place was saving me. It was sacred, a sanctuary unto itself and it was helping my tears to stop flowing.

I let them dry on my face as I looked down at the binders full of Lil's poorly kept records. I opened up my spreadsheets and files to where I had left off earlier that day and forced my attention, every last ounce of it, on the task at hand.

I couldn't think about my problems right now. I needed to think about Lil's, and as much as it broke my heart to admit it, there were some whoppers.

The numbers never seemed to add up to what I wanted them to. It wasn't like she was going under or anything. It wasn't like she was running her business poorly, well unless you included proper and organized record keeping in "running your business." That she could definitely improve on.

No, the problem came when I tried to find ways to make more of a profit. The problem came with finding money for Drew's college fund. I had run through every possible scenario and the only things I could think of, Lil wouldn't like.

They would have to cut back significantly on staff or start charging more. A cover fee for Thursday nights might be beneficial but I already could hear Lil's voice protesting. She would probably say something like "Music is food for the soul and soul food should be free."

I didn't want to be the one that cut into the charm and culture of the place but if she wanted to find some way to pay for Drew to go to school without the help of loans, she was going to have to do something. I looked down at the books again to try and find other places to cut or change but if felt like I was trying to zip this place up in a dress that didn't fit.

The zipper wouldn't close.

I had to find a way though and tonight of all nights, I was bound and determined to do just that.

I kept working, shifting my gaze from papers to the computer screen until I heard a soft knock on the door. I knew who it was before I looked up.

"Hey, Quinn," I said.

"I knew I'd find you doing something like this. Lil did too because she told me where her office was before I even asked." Quinn responded.

"Am I that easy to read?"

"Mmm, I just think that Lil and I are especially in tune."

"You kind of are," I said with a little laugh. "Maybe that's why I liked her. Because she reminds me a little bit of you. That and the rocket ship."

"Yeah I noticed that too. What's that all about?" Quinn asked as she pulled a chair from the corner closer to the desk.

"Lil did it for her son, Drew because he loved space when he was a kid. It's a long, beautiful story but that wasn't what drew me here. I mean it would have had I known it at the time but really, I just saw the place and knew it was somewhere that Ollie would want to be. With its charm and quirks and uniqueness you know?" I said with a small smile. Tears were filling my eyes again.

"I thought the same thing when I got here Wills. It's funny how it worked out, isn't it? The way that you found him here, miles away?"

"Yeah I guess I did."

"Actually, it's not all that funny. It's not surprising anyway."

"Why not?" I asked in confusion. I had put my papers down at this point, shifted my attention to my sister.

"Because Willa, you carry him inside your heart. He's there and that's where he belongs. But here's the thing, don't let that piece of him take over the rest of you. Don't let it turn your whole heart into sadness or cloud your hopes of something else."

"Is that why you think I came back here?"

"Partly," she said it calmly, with knowing composure. "The other part was because Jacob gave you such a cold reception out there."

"Especially in tune, you are," I said in my best impression of Yoda.

"Yeah I saw it but what I also saw was how he watched you

walk out. I saw how sad he looked and the way that he started banging all of his gear around like he was frustrated at himself. I also saw the way Lil shook her head at him and then she turned to me and said 'Valentine's Day is hard on them both then isn't it?'"

"Really? He did that? I asked with too much hope in my voice.

"Yes," Quinn said in a slow drawn out voice.

I smiled for a minute but then my frustration and confusion returned. "Well, so what. He still seemed like he wanted nothing to do with me when I was actually there. And why is Valentine's Day hard for him? I'm the one with the dead fiancé!" I knew I sounded petulant but it was Quinn. I could just be who I was and all would be well.

"Yes, you are and that's why I'm here but maybe, just maybe, he has some baggage of his own. Plus, from what it sounds like, you didn't exactly encourage him this morning. Can you just afford him some grace Wills?"

I looked down at my work again without responding. I didn't know how to respond. Should I do what Quinn wanted or should I cling to the past? The one with Ollie where it was ok to be sad and lonely, where I had an excuse to be sheltered and to feel what I wanted and to not consider why other people do the things they do or feel the things they feel.

She let me stay like that and we sat in companionable silence for a moment. My fingers clicked on the keyboard and she pulled a nail file out of her purse. We sounded like a percussion section with our clicks and scrapes. I had just begun to settle into our rhythm when music, real, live, perfect music poured in from the café just outside the office door.

Jacob sang. His voice poured in as warm and rich and dark as melted chocolate.

It flowed into my sanctuary and it made my heart ache in all the right ways. As much as I didn't want to, I let it pour over me and warm me. It thawed and melted the cold places, the lonely places, and it fed my soul.

I knew that my heart was a mess. I knew that I didn't know anything about it right now, that I had one arm grasping for Ollie and the other reaching for someone new all while the rest of me balked at the idea and hurt and desperation of love.

But there it was, love. Not that I was in love but there was the promise of it. The song about it. The feel of it in the room. Maybe it stemmed from my giving way to thinking about someone else, to thinking about where Jacob was coming from. Maybe it stemmed from Quinn's suggestion of grace but it was there all the same.

Love was good. I had known it once and it was good. I would treasure that and maybe, someday, I would know it again.

Chapter 11

Jacob

I met Jenny the week after my Dad died. I remember how everything felt, or really, how it didn't feel. It was like I had been living in a fog for days. Nothing was in color anymore. Nothing tasted right. It was all just a sepia-toned world and nothing I could do could snap me out of it.

I couldn't picture my life without him. It seemed like I was a boat without a sail, just floating and going nowhere. He and I talked almost every day and not just about sports or weather or cars. No, we really, really talked about everything. There wasn't a girl that I liked or a grade that I got or a joke that I laughed at that he didn't know about. He was my best friend in the world because we were the same, he and I. He knew what I was going to say before I said it but still, he listened with everything he had in him and then always gave a wise, thoughtful answer.

He's the reason that I became a counselor and I swear to you that I draw on how he lived and how he listened more than any of the schooling I received when I see my patients. That's why I felt so lost. I had lost my father, my friend, and my guide all in one fell swoop and the future looked meaningless and scary and far too big for me to handle.

I had tried to increase my hours at the gym, thinking maybe that if I pushed my muscles, felt the burn of lactic acid and the endorphins flooding my being, then I might feel alive again. All it did was leave me buzzing even more. Like there was energy trapped inside me but it couldn't get out. I knew that's what it was; trapped because I was trapped. All of me, stuck, held fast by shock and grief and panic and anger.

When that didn't work, I went to a party, the first and only party that I had ever been to. Some fraternity hosted it and I only knew about it because my roommate had seen a flyer somewhere. It was raucous and loud and dripping with some unknown liquor. Dripping with that and girls, everywhere. I dove headfirst into the pool of it all, guzzling down whatever I could find and kissing whoever was willing but even then, it was all nothing, meaningless, it didn't even begin to touch the pain and the numbness that I felt simultaneously. The only thing that felt right was the throwing up at the end of the night. Finally, a bodily reaction that mirrored how I felt, sick and poisoned and past my limit.

I just couldn't get it all out of my head. The phone call from Lil, the way I could hear and feel her sobs through the phone. The way that Drew had clung to my hand through the whole funeral, not letting go even to grab a cookie at the reception afterward. The way that my Dad had looked lying in that casket. He was wearing a suit and tie which I had seen him do maybe twice in my whole life and his skin looked like pleather; fake and stretched shiny thin over his frame. None of it was right.

It had haunted me for days because it had all been so sudden but I guess that's what heart attacks are; sudden. It wouldn't be called an attack if it wasn't a sudden, spontaneous, stealthy thing. Like in a war when the ramparts are seized and cities are sacked, our family had been overtaken before we were even given a white flag to raise.

So, I walked around my college campus in a daze, going through the motions and eating because people told me to. That is until I saw Jenny.

She was sitting with a group of girls under a tree in the park across the street from campus and they were all circled around her like she was the teacher and they were the students. She had blonde hair that glowed like a pot of gold at the end of a rainbow and I sat there thinking that she very much was that very thing. She seemed to be a treasure that I had spotted after a storm. She flicked her hair and turned her face towards the sun and I saw her perfectly rounded cheeks and dimpled chin, her bright blue eyes that looked like jewels crowning an hourglass figure.

She was undeniably beautiful in a siren sort of way and I felt like Odysseus, drawn to the song of her laughter and lure of her eyes. If my Dad had been there, he would have grounded me, bound me to the mast like Odysseus' men. He would have seen from yards away that she had that look in her eyes, one of lust but not love, one of selfishness and not sacrifice. He would have turned me away, gently but firmly and reminded me that beauty is revealed in a person's character and not in their outward appearance. He would have told me not to let myself fall so hard and so fast. But there I stood, alone and unfettered and I drifted to her like a piece of wood on the water.

It's odd really when I look back on it because the way I was with her was not the way I had ever been before. I'm reserved and calculated by nature but with her, things were different.

She saw me from that tree in the park and she walked right over to me, standing on the steps of The Student Union and she said this:

"You look like you're thinking about kissing me, am I right?" Her blue eyes flashed with a sparkle that bespoke confidence and anticipation. She knew what she was doing and she was excited by her ability to do it.

I didn't know what to do because she was in fact, perfectly right. That's exactly what I was thinking and I blushed at the fact that it was so obvious. All I could manage was a smile and a nod.

"Why don't you take me to dinner tonight and we can see if your daydreams come true."

I cleared my throat and managed an "Ok." And she handed me her phone number with a wink.

"Call soon to make plans. I don't like to eat anywhere without a reservation." And then she walked off, confident that I would do her bidding, which of course I did.

From then on, I followed her like a puppy dog, pleased to live in her shadow and follow her orders. I didn't think I had any other choice really because she was the only thing in the world that seemed to make me feel again after I had lost my Dad. She seemed to make the world come alive again. She seemed to paint it all in her own colors, colors that were brighter and more flashy than anything I had seen before. It was like she lived in a world that flashed neon signs while everyone else used candlelight. It mesmerized me and woke me up and I lived and fed off of her energy.

I didn't care what I had to do to make her happy. I did it all. Drove her places, bought her gifts, cleaned her car, anything because I owed her my happiness. At least that's what I thought.

It took me years to realize that I was wrong.

Even in the rocky landscape of a relationship that followed, I wouldn't acknowledge that she was wrong for me. She knew we weren't anything worth chasing but I must have made it worth her while to keep coming back because that's what she would do. She would leave me heartbroken for a month or two and then come back and always, always, I was waiting.

She must have seen that I was clinging to her like a Band-Aid, that she was my medication but she didn't do anything to stop it. Probably because she was the type of person that saw herself as the sun and everyone else as the world, just orbiting around her, pulled into her gravity and light. It fed her hot and scorching confidence. She never stopped me from waiting for her and adoring her because it fueled her and she must have felt that it was ok because she was fueling me right back.

I used to ask her what she did, who she saw when we were on our countless "breaks" but she would always just say "Let's leave it in the past Jake. I'm with you now aren't I?" And I would because I couldn't push her, push her to answer or push her away. I needed her to make my world turn and the lights to stay on or the darkness of grief that I had avoided would take over and I would realize how lost I was.

This went on for years, all through Drew's illness and the rigmarole of college and grad school. I clung to her but she never clung back and I never saw it. She was the one sunbathing on the raft of our relationship, easy and free while I was in the water kicking and panting while I pushed along against the current.

That's why when it ended and she turned me down for my old roommate, I was left floundering. Not just because I had lost her, but because I had lost my Dad years before and had never dealt with it.

I had lost everything that I had clung to and my hands were left empty. I remember staring down at them in the weeks after we broke up for the final time squinting hard. I felt like I should see rope burn, red and angry on my palms because it felt like I had been clinging to a rope that was ripped from me hard and fast.

I realized, of course, that I had been self-medicating with her.

That the root of my issues would be addressed when I truly let myself grieve for my father and that's what I did.

Lil was thrilled by it. By the breakup and the acknowledging of my grief. Not because she delighted in my pain but because she had been praying for my healing and it was finally coming.

A week after Jenny left me, Lil sat me down and forced me to watch home movies of us as kids. Films of birthday parties and Christmas and running through the sprinklers. Shots of my dad tickling us and popping up out of a giant present with two puppies in his arms. Pictures of him holding me while I slept with my baseball glove still on or of him twirling Lil around the kitchen. It was all good. It was all necessary and we cried right there on the couch.

The healing came slowly and surely, like spring or the sunrise and eventually, I dealt with his death and my loss. That I can say, I've done but the rest? The part where I had to acknowledge the heartbreak of love lost and dreams of romance crushed. The section of my heart that had been used and abused and burned by Jenny's selfishness and neglect. The soft spot that every man has that yearns to be loved and admired. That, I hadn't looked at.

I shut it up tight and locked the door. I let it harden over and suffocated the hope because, well, I had tried that once and it didn't work. What would make me think it ever would?

* * *

"I want to talk to you," Lil said as she stood in the doorway of my office. I was between clients and somehow she knew. No doubt Angie had told her. I looked over Lil's shoulder and saw that very woman eating one of Lil's gigantic chocolate chip cookies with a look of bliss on her face.

"You bought your way in here didn't you?" I asked.

"That I did. Don't worry I brought you one too."

She set a paper bag with the Aurora Boreal Inn and Café logo on it down on my desk along with a cup of coffee. I smelled the two and imagined the pairing of sweet milk chocolate and her dark coffee. My resolve was faltering.

"Fine," I said with a sigh. "I've got a minute. Come on in."

Lil was already situating herself on the couch across from my desk. She sat down and folded her legs up underneath her while she hugged one of my pillows to her chest. It was the same position she would assume when we were growing up and she had pushed her way into my bedroom after I got home from a date. Like she was getting comfy because she knew that somehow, she was going to force a nice long story out of me.

I took a drink of the coffee and pulled the cookie out in preparation for the support that I knew I would need.

The fact of the matter was that I had been expecting this visit for a while now. I had been avoiding the café for about a week and I knew it wouldn't go unnoticed.

"We haven't seen you in a while," she said it like it was a question.

"Yeah, I've just been busy is all," I said through a bite of cookie.

"Well, that's just not true."

"How do you know that?"

"Because I checked your schedule with Angie and you haven't been any busier than normal."

"That woman cannot be trusted," I said under my breath.

"Oh yes, she can," Lil said as she waved off my comment. "She cares about you and so do I and we're working in tandem. Anyone that's working with me can be trusted."

"Jake, I know why you haven't been around and you know why you haven't been around so why don't you just come out and say it so we can get past it all."

I sighed in exasperation but didn't respond beyond that.

"Fine. I'll say it. You've been avoiding the café because you don't want to run into Willa. Is that it? She seemed disinterested which hurt you so you aren't coming around?"

"Lil, it's not as dramatic as all that. I'm not that sensitive. I'm just keeping my distance so I don't fan any feelings that I'm trying to smother." I looked down at my desk and pulled out a notebook. I pretended to write something down and then I shuffled through some papers. Busy work.

"Well, I think that's a pretty dumb idea if you ask me."

I looked up at her with a scowl and shook my head.

"Jake, I know you. I know that what happened with Jenny broke a piece of your soul and now you're running scared but I also know that there's more to Willa than we realize and I really, truly think that the two of you could be some kind of balm for each other."

"Not now Lil," I said.

"Yes now! I'm your big sister and I'm sick and tired of watching you hurt! Sure you put on a happy face, you even find joy in the things in your life but you're lonely Jake and you're hurting. Your heart is still hurting and it kills me!" Her voice caught on the end of her sentence, like the lump of tears had a sharp edge that snagged her words and unraveled them. She paused for a minute and wiped the tears away from her cheeks. I watched and waited, giving her my full attention.

Finally, she took in a ragged sigh. "Jacob, you got us through, you know that? You carried us on your back all through Drew's cancer and opening the business. I'll never forget the day you moved out of your dorm room, gave up your whole college experience to come live with us. I saw how your buddies all gave you hugs while they teased you for leaving. How the girls from your hall looked at you like the one that got away. You didn't even *notice,* though! You didn't even see the way that they all missed you and wanted you there with them, probably to make them laugh and pick them up from a party when they were drunk. They all knew the man you were and they felt your absence. You didn't even look back, though. You just put Drew on your shoulders and said 'Well, what's for dinner Lil?' You gave up your once in a lifetime chance for all that; your fan club and your memories for *us* and I'll never, ever, not in a million years be able to pay you back for all of it..."

"There's nothing to pay back Lil..."

"Yes, there is! We owe you everything so I can't stand by with a debt like that hanging over my head and watch a blessing pass you by. I can't watch the cure to your loneliness go."

"We don't know that that's what she is. I thought Jenny could be that for me but she wasn't," I said quietly.

"Well, you were wrong as you could ever be with her. She was the worst and I always said so," she said with fire in her voice.

I couldn't help but laugh at the way that she changed her mood from tender and affectionate sister to a vengeful one full of hatred.

"Yeah, Drew told me," I said.

"I'm glad he still remembers what I said about her because if he ever brought anyone home like that, it would kill me."

"Me too," I said. I couldn't imagine Drew falling in love with someone who was so careless with other people's feelings, so selfish, so wrong.

"This is the problem though Jake! Every time we talk about love, she comes up! I hate that. I don't want her associated with it! I want you to have a relationship that can replace those memories, really that can displace them because that can't be your experience!" She was desperate now.

"I want you to fall for someone good and kind who loves hard and well so that you can get the proper idea of love into that thick skull of yours. I want more for you. Better for you. A man that's as good and selfless and smart and kind... you deserve it all Jake." She was crying again and I couldn't help but go over to the couch and give her a one armed hug.

"What do you want me to do, sis?" I asked gently.

"I want you to stop running. I want you to stop holding on to that horrible woman and what she did to you and let whatever is going to happen happen so that you can move on. I want you to find joy."

"For you," I said reluctantly. "I'll try for you."

"Great!" she said. "I know just where we'll start."

* * *

The plan was to meet at the café at 10 am on Saturday. Lil had decided that that would give us enough time to finish up before lunch. Why it needed to be before lunch was beyond me. Probably because meals were sacred to Lil, and in her mind, you could miss those as easily as a nun could miss church. Either way, though, that was the plan.

I had no idea why I had agreed to help. Well, actually I did. Despite my misgivings and attempts to get over Willa, I was still the same man that my father had raised-decent and kind and when a person needs help, I give it. According to Lil, Willa did need help so I was bound by common decency and my sister's all knowing and all persuading eyes to be there.

We; Drew, Lil, Willa, and I were going to be moving her stuff into a storage unit. She had left it in a small moving trailer parked outside of Lil's unused garage for the last few months so it was about time to do something about it. I mean, it made sense to do something about it but the timing of this whole endeavor seemed to fit better with some scheme that Lil had cooked up than with common sense.

So, there I was, standing outside on the porch of the Aurora

Boreal Inn and Café waiting for everyone else to meet me. There was a chill in the air, the kind that lingers in spring. I could tell that snow might be in the forecast later but right now, it was tolerable enough to stay outside and enjoy the fresh air. I sat down in one of the rocking chairs and began to mindlessly move back and forth, back and forth, trying to rock my misgivings to sleep. At least for the morning.

It had been two weeks since I had seen Willa and in that time, I had convinced myself that what I had interpreted as interest within myself was not. It was a childish crush on a woman I knew next to nothing about. Well, that is except for her heart. I had gotten to see that pretty plainly on more than one occasion and it seemed like a complicated, beautiful, maze of a mess. One that had hooked me a little too soon.

Today, though, I wouldn't let it. I was here to lift boxes into a storage unit and that was it. Nothing more, nothing less. Manual labor. I could do that. We could be two adults who are in each other's lives in a purely platonic way. We could be friends. We were friends and this was the kind of thing that friends did for each other. Move stuff. I sat in the rocking chair, convincing myself into the friend zone until…

"Oh, hi Jacob." Her voice floated over from the doorway like a breeze and it left me feeling tousled.

"Willa," I said evenly. I looked at her but tried to keep my guard up. When I made eye contact with her, though, I could see how nervous she was, that she was uncomfortable and it cooled my reserve just slightly.

She cleared her throat and there was a pause for just a minute until she said. "Thanks so much for helping today. You didn't have to."

She was looking down at her shoes now, pink tennis shoes with white polka dots on them. They looked playful and I wondered when the last time she felt like that was. The idea of it, of a carefree and laughing Willa, made my heart beat a little faster, it made me want to bring that out in her. It had to be there. She wouldn't pick shoes like that if it wasn't.

"I like your shoes," I said, trying to ease the tension. She was still uneasy, though, still looking down at her shoes, not at me.

"Oh, yeah these? I thought they were fun. I bought them a few months ago as a little pick me up. Polka dots can do that don't you think? Well, you probably haven't really ever thought much about polka dots, have you? Why would you? Men don't wear them. Actually, you probably don't even understand the idea of buying shoes as a pick me up. Retail therapy and polka dots are definitely feminine things. Especially when you combine the two..."

"Willa, why are you nervous?" I interrupted her rambling, a sure sign that she was uncomfortable. I was looking at her now, her face and not her shoes. I knew that I was to blame for this awkwardness and I couldn't bear it. We were adults. We could say what needed to be said and move on.

"Well," she said and then cleared her throat, "It's just that I haven't seen you in a while and I was worried it was because of Valentine's Day."

"What about Valentine's Day?" I asked. I knew, but I wanted to hear her take.

"All of it really. That morning, I think I misread your tone and the way you looked at me and maybe I took it to mean more than it did. And then, in my classic fashion, I freaked out a little bit and made something completely normal into something awkward."

"You mean the way you reacted to me?"

"Yes. I was short and cold after you were being perfectly nice. It wasn't your fault. It's just coming from the place that I've been in for the last few years. It's not a good place mind you, and it causes me to react to things in a way that's different than I used to," She shook her head like she had gotten off track and said: "Never mind that, I was wrong and rude but then..."

"What?"

"Well, I had planned to be better that night after I had thought everything through and talked to Quinn and had all that chocolate but then you wanted nothing to do with me and haven't ever since." She fluttered her hands around while she talked like they were puppets, telling a story all their own. Like she was throwing her voice into them like a ventriloquist and I was mesmerized by the whole thing.

"I'm just kind of confused is all Jacob. I don't really know what to make of our interactions because, maybe I'm wrong but I sensed something building for a little bit, even just a friendship but it feels like something happened and I don't know what. If it was the way I talked to you, then I'm so sorry."

"Look, Willa, we are friends. I'm here, aren't I?" I knew I should say more. Maybe accept her apology or go one better and tell her it wasn't even necessary. She had said something, though; that something had happened and she didn't know what and she was right. Something had happened that had nothing to do with her and because of her, I was realizing that I still needed to find my way out of it.

She looked me in the eye for a second and narrowed hers ever so slightly. "Do you want to be here Jacob?" She asked.

Did I? I had been doing everything I could to avoid her for two weeks but deep down, I knew that I did.

I looked at her then, right in the eyes and we held each other's gaze for a long minute. There were words I wanted to say, stories I wanted to tell, to make her understand where I was at and where I wanted to be but all of them had to be left alone for now. For now, all I could do was respond with "Yes."

We waited there on the porch for a quiet minute and then she crossed and sat in the chair next to mine. We rocked in silence in alternating rhythms, her chair forward while mine was back and vice versa. We were rocking in different directions but somehow the whole of it, her chair and mine, formed completion, leaving no space unfilled. When I couldn't be in one direction, she was there and when she couldn't, I was. It was simple but beautiful and my hesitancy about being with her faded ever so slightly.

"I think rocking chairs are the grown up version of swings," Willa said. "I think that the person who invented them realized that it just wasn't fair that kids could sit down and go back and forth and back and forth until they were hypnotized by the world in front of them so they made these." She rubbed the arm of her chair affectionately and smiled as she looked around the porch.

"I think rocking chairs probably came first," I said.

"Well, there's no need to have a chicken or the egg conversation right now, Jacob," she said as she pulled her shoulders back and flicked her hair and I suppressed a laugh.

"We're ok now, aren't we?" she said matter of factly.

"We are," I said with a slow nod.

"Good, because there are a lot of heavy things to lift and I need you."

She smiled at me, a sight that was slowly becoming more prevalent and it reminded me of her polka dots. It was unexpected but seemed to fit right in on her. The last two weeks had been a waste. I wanted this person, this dramatic, stubborn, emotional, beautiful person in my life and today was a good day to dive back in. That is if she was willing to let me…

Chapter 12

Willa

It was time.

I had been avoiding that trailer full of my stuff for weeks now and it was time to stop. I hadn't wanted to stop avoiding it for a couple of reasons. First of all, I hadn't wanted to see it all. I knew what was in there; the things that I couldn't part with when I left Austin, the things that held memories like a vacuum holds dust. I knew that when the time came to look at it all again, things might be a little tough. A lot of tough actually, and I had somehow gotten to a place here in Colorado where those tough moments were fewer and farther between.

The second reason had to do with that; with Colorado. Unpacking my trailer of stuff meant that I was going to be staying here.

I wanted to stay here. That I knew well enough. I had established enough of a business to feel supported and I loved the people here. The mountains were beautiful and the weather was great. It was as good a place as any to settle down and let my roots grow a bit but still, it meant that I was officially building and cultivating a life that Ollie would never know anything about. As crazy as it may sound, I thought about the fact that if some crazy sci-fi, rom-com miracle happened and he came back to life, he wouldn't recognize my days. He wouldn't find anything familiar in my life and that was a little bit sad.

I knew that he would find this idea utterly hilarious and ridiculous. I did too but still, all of it combined; seeing my old stuff and putting that old stuff, the pieces of my old life into a physical space in my new life was weird, to say the least.

I didn't really know how to verbalize this when Lil had approached me about it, though.

"So Willa, how long do you think we'll get to have that trailer of yours parked here?" She had asked a few days before. I could sense her jest but also the seriousness behind her question.

"Yeah, sorry about that Lil. I guess I just didn't know what to do with it. I'm still not sure what I want to do about a permanent living situation here. Do I go apartment or house you know? And I didn't really think about doing anything with it until then." That was the best I could come up with. Lil did me one better, though.

"What do you mean permanent? This is as permanent a place as you want it to be. You don't have to leave anytime soon," she said.

"Really?" I asked, surprised. I hadn't realized it until she had offered that I stay but I wanted to stay. I didn't want to live anywhere else. Alone. I think that Lil knew that. She sensed my needs and moods like she always did.

"Sure! You're still working for me and this time of year, I don't need as many rooms so make yourself at home by moving that ugly trailer out of here!" she said with a smile.

I laughed and said, "Ok but I promise, I'll be gone eventually. Do you know of any storage units around here?"

We made plans from there which led me to the moment on

the porch with Jacob and then all the moments after that in the car with him, Lil, and Drew and then at the storage unit.

We began to unload my trailer box by box.

Because I had packed it all, every box was labeled with a list of its contents in alphabetical order. It was a system that I had spent hours cultivating and the project of all of it had been so therapeutic for me. I had a task, a tedious task to take my mind off of my grief and the second that we opened the trailer door and saw all of the neatly labeled boxes with my perfectly straight lines of tape and alphabetical order, I remembered the thoroughness that I had completed the task of packing with. It was a beautiful sight of order and control to me. I had put all of those boxes inside that trailer and thought to myself "Well, at least my stuff is perfectly organized and sorted. Now, maybe my life will follow." This trailer had been my mental projection, the embodiment of all of my hopes for the future. That soon, everything in my life would be as tidy as that trailer.

To me, it made sense but to the other three there, it was a marvel, one worthy of admiration and laughter.

"Umm, Willa, I'm going to need you to explain to me how something like this happens." Lil said with wide eyes as she waved her hands in front of the open trailer door. "Never in my life, have I seen such order and perfection and I don't know what affect it might have on me. It could be my kryptonite you know?"

"It will be for sure." Jacob said with a laugh. "I think if you get any closer, your messy disorganized self might be in danger of being transformed by the power of order and organization. Stand back!"

"It's not that bad is it?" I asked with a laugh.

"Willa, this is a work of packing art. I've never seen such meticulously labeled boxes stacked in such perfect rows." Lil said.

"Yeah, you should see my mom pack. I won't get into too many details but I'll just let you know that we use trash bags instead of boxes and NONE of them are labeled," Drew said as he got a little closer to read the contents of the boxes.

"Well, to each his own I guess. This is just how I like to do it," I said with a shrug. "That way, there's no guessing while you unpack."

"Right," Jacob said as he grabbed a box. "Well, I'm going to get started by moving your, let's see, colander, pans, pots, lids, skillet, and spatulas."

"And I'm going to grab your blankets, comforter, pillows, and sheets," Drew said.

"I've got the vases, bowls, and plates," Lil said loudly.

We all paused for a second and then I said, "That's not what I wrote is it? In that order?"

"Nope. I just had to put my stamp on it. I scrambled them."

"Ha. Ha," I said with a smile. "Just don't scramble the box itself, that stuff is fragile."

We went on like that for a while, reading off the list of things in each box, Drew, Jacob and I in alphabetical order, Lil in whatever order pleased her. Sometimes she would read the words backwards. Other times in Pig Latin, other times in no order whatsoever.

It was nice, it really was, because it was *light*. The whole process was light. I mean, the boxes were still heavy but there, reading off my ridiculous alphabetical lists, I was able to acknowledge the contents of my old life with ease and humor. With people that I had grown to love.

Box after box was transferred from the trailer to the storage unit that was a little closet of a thing just behind the hardware store in town until we were almost done. Only a few things remained. Jacob, Drew, and I were moving some things around inside the unit to make room for what was left when Lil appeared in the door holding a long rectangular box. I knew what it was and my heart dropped a few notches. Lil looked at me with concern in her eyes.

A million questions and a million feelings were there in her look.

"Wedding Dress," she said quietly and she held it out to me like it was a gift.

Jacob looked over sharply at Lil and me with a furrow in his brow. I looked between the two of them and knew that it was time. It was time to talk about it. To lay it all out so I could finally, once and for all, begin again here in this new place.

"Is this a family heirloom, Willa?" Lil asked hesitantly.

"No, it's mine. Well, it was mine. I mean, it still is but I never wore it," I said. I was surprised that I hadn't started crying yet, I told myself to give it time.

"Why not?" Jacob asked gently.

"Because," I said as I took it gingerly from Lil's outstretched hands. "My fiancé died a week after I bought it."

I saw the light go out of their eyes. I felt the air leave the space. It was exactly what I was worried would happen. People never know what to say to people who have lost someone. They just stand there, awkwardly wondering which platitude to choose. "I'm sorry," or "He's in a better place," Or "You'll be together again someday," And then the grieving person is left feeling guilty for inviting awkwardness to the party and so they clear their throat and put on a smile and try to change the subject by feigning a deep and undying interest in the weather or how the other person's mother is.

That's what I was just about to do but before I could paste the smile on, Lil walked over to me, took the box from my hands, set it down, and pulled me into a hug. A big, strong, soft, all-encompassing hug.

We stayed like that for what felt like five whole minutes, her holding me and imparting peace and love through her embrace. It wasn't awkward or uncomfortable. It felt right. Like Lil needed to do this as much as I did and I leaned into it, surrendered to it, and silently thanked her for stopping me from saying that it was ok that she had just handed me the dress I should have worn to marry a man that I had to bury.

Finally, she pulled away and with tears in her eyes, she said "I bet it's got lace on it, doesn't it? You would look beautiful in white lace."

My eyes filled with tears then too and I said. "Yes, it's lace from head to toe."

"What was his name?" Lil asked.

"Oliver but no one ever called him that. He was Ollie. He was always Ollie," I said with a smile through my tears.

"What happened?" Came Jacob's voice from behind me. It was deep and sorrowful, like a dark blue blanket or a cozy night sky enveloping me.

"There was a car crash. He had just opened a photography studio that displayed pictures from up and coming artists in Austin. He loved it, everything about it and he was working late that night to finish an exhibit for a show the next day. Anyway, he was on his way home and so was a drunk driver. They say he died on impact and that he didn't suffer. I know they told me that to comfort me so I wouldn't stay awake at night picturing him struggling to be ok only to die alone in that crushed car. Still, there's only so much solace you can find in the way someone you love dies. Nothing can make it better, not even the fact that he didn't suffer because maybe he didn't but I did for a long time."

I paused for a minute remembering the earliest, darkest moments and then my eyes landed on the dress.

"I got a call six weeks after he died that my dress had come in. I had ordered it before everything happened and had forgotten to cancel it. For some crazy reason, I went to the boutique in a daze and picked it up. The lady smiled at me and told me what a beautiful bride I would be and that I had picked such a lovely dress. She asked when the wedding would be and I told her we had picked the

21st night of September."

"She said, 'Like the song?' and I said 'Yep!' with fake joy and bravado. I smiled and thanked her and let myself pretend that everything was normal and ok for just a minute. I let myself walk out of that bridal boutique like the bride I wanted to be with a pasted on, half hysterical smile but as soon as I got to the car, it all fell away. Like Cinderella leaving the ball at midnight you know? I turned my car in the direction of the nearest dry cleaners, took the dress in, and had them box it up and preserve it. I hadn't even put it on but there was something morbidly fulfilling in the fact that if Ollie had to be stuck in a lifeless box for the rest of my life, so would this dress. I don't know why I kept it, or why I brought it with me but I did, and here we are."

Everyone was silent for a minute, letting the story sink in.

"I love that song," Lil finally said.

"What?" I asked.

"September!" she said.

"Oh! Yeah, it was Ollie's favorite. He loved Earth, Wind, and Fire. We were going to dance our first dance to that song," I said with a wistful smile.

Lil looked at me and smiled. She grabbed my hand and then, out of nowhere, she started singing.

Every word of "September" began to pour out of her mouth. She was the megaphone and the music all at once and it bellowed and boomed off of the storage unit walls. She started singing louder and clapping her hands. It was a little off tune but her rhythm was good and she began to dance around the small space, filling it with music and joy.

She paused for a minute and wagged her eyebrows at me before she grabbed my hands and spun me as she sang

Drew started playing a beat on the boxes behind me and made horn sounds with his mouth. As the "instruments" grew louder, Lil matched them with her singing. Louder she sang, the whole song word for word.

And she spun me until I was laughing harder than I had in years.

I was drunk on that laughter. Giddy with it, electrified by it. There in the room fragrant with my story of how I had lost Ollie, we danced and laughed to his favorite song. All while my new friends and my old wedding dress watched. It was poetic and cheesy and utterly beautiful all at once.

At the end of it all, Lil and I collapsed on the floor in puddles of laughter and lost breath and Jacob applauded from the corner. I looked over at him and saw that he had tears in his eyes while he smiled and clapped. I stopped laughing then but my smile stayed on my face as I fought to catch my breath. We locked eyes and for a minute nothing was said but then he changed that.

"You did it, Willa. You danced."

I nodded and said, "I did!"

"It was beautiful." And then he turned away to continue arranging my boxes. To make room for me to stay.

Chapter 13

Willa

"That was some story you told us back there," Jacob said between bites of soup.

We had gone back to the Café for lunch after the storage unit was filled to bursting with my memories, both the physical and the spoken. Lil was rushing around serving her customers all things warm on this chilly afternoon while Drew did the same and Jacob and I sat in a cozy corner booth with warm bowls of chicken and wild rice soup and steaming hot bread between us.

"You think so?" I asked.

"I do. I know I didn't say much then but I want you to know that I heard you. I heard your story and I'm glad to know it. I'm glad to know where you came from," Jacob replied. He wiped his mouth with his napkin and began to butter a crusty piece of French bread.

"You know what? After spending a few months here and finally feeling like this could be home, I was glad to tell you all," I said and I meant it.

"You feel like this could be home?" Jacob asked. It was so like him to zero in on the part of my sentence that I didn't really think about, the truth that was shared unintentionally.

"Why do you do that?" I asked.

"Do what?"

"Find the thing that I said that I didn't mean to say and then ask me about it."

"You didn't mean to say that this feels like home to you?"

"No, I mean, I didn't say it by accident. It's fine that I said it. It's just, the point that I was trying to get across was that I was glad I talked to you all about everything. Not that this place feels like home," I said.

I tried to take a bite of my bread in as lady like a way as possible since he was watching me with that undivided attention he so often gave. I decided that it would be too crumbly to put the thing in my mouth when my hand was half way there and settled on tearing it instead. That didn't help much, though. I still managed to get crumbs all over my lap and the table in the process. I must have looked like a complete idiot. One who had never eaten bread before. I briefly began to think about diagnosing myself with a gluten intolerance just to spare myself from the crumbly embarrassment I was going through at the moment but Jacob spoke before I let myself get too far down that road.

"I didn't realize I was doing anything. That's just what stood out to me when you spoke. That you felt at home. That's a powerful statement," he said with a smile. He watched me brush the crumbs off of my lap as I chewed a bite of my bread. Thank God I hadn't lied about a gluten intolerance. It was delicious. While I chewed, I thought about what he said. Home was a powerful word. He was right.

"The word 'home' is a good word. It's just plain good. And

that's how I feel when I'm here in the café or with Lil or Drew or, even you. I'm grateful because I haven't felt like that since I was with Ollie."

"He was your home," Jacob said matter of factly between bites of soup.

"Yes. He was. And I've been homeless ever since he died. That's why I came here."

Jacob nodded and said, "How did you pick this place anyway?"

"I didn't. My gas tank did. I said that I would stay at whatever place I was after I ran out of three tanks of gas."

He laughed at me, a rich, comforting sound like waves washing up on the beach. "I guess that's as good a plan as any," he said.

"I thought it was. I thought it was very dramatic and poetic actually," I said with my best pistol pose.

"You like drama and poetry, don't you?" He asked with a half smile.

"Of course, I do."

"What else?" He asked as he took another bite of soup.

"What do you mean?" I said as I took one too.

"I mean, what else do you like? Tell me more about yourself."

"There's not much to tell," I said with a shrug.

"Sure there is. Come on."

"I don't know... I haven't been interested in all that much since Ollie died."

It was true. I had spent most of my time missing him. That was my hobby, my obsession, who I was.

He looked at me for a minute as if weighing his words but then he said them. Oh, did he say them!

"There's more there, Willa. There's more to you than Ollie," he said it gently but his voice was strong. His words were strong and they hit me like cold water in the face.

And that's how I reacted. Like cold water had been thrown at my face. Like he had just reached across the table with his glass of ice water and flung it at me. Never mind the kindness in his eyes, his professional experience with seeing the situation and telling people what they needed to hear. Never mind the good place that we had arrived at that day. Never mind the fact that he was one hundred percent, wholly, and completely right. I erupted.

"You don't understand Jacob. You don't get how I feel or where I'm at or even who I am because I don't. I don't know who I am without him! I've loved Ollie since high school. I've loved him longer than I've loved red wine or shopping online or falling asleep with the TV on. I grew up and became who I am all while I loved him and then he was gone and I didn't know who I was. My cornerstone was ripped out from under me and I feel like I've been tipping over ever since. Like I'm about to fall and become a pile of rubble. Like I can't stand on my own without him! When he died, I didn't just lose him, I lost me."

The tears were streaming down full force now. The geyser had erupted and there was no stopping it. He had triggered something in me, had pushed just close enough to launch the sequence that I had been trying to smother, the one that would let me acknowledge everything that was beneath the lid of my heart.

"Willa, you're right. I don't know exactly how you feel. I mean, I don't know how it feels to bury your fiancé but I do know how it feels to lose people you love and to lose yourself and your plans in the process."

"You do?" I asked. "How?"

"I'm not all that young, Willa. I've been in relationships before. I've been in love," he said looking down at his hands with a self-deprecating smile and a shrug.

"Well, of course. I didn't mean to imply..." I said embarrassed, he was disarming me quickly and I knew it.

"No, you didn't imply anything. It's fine," He waved his hand in the air, brushing aside my comments.

"So what happened? How did you lose someone?" I asked shyly, hedging my bets that he would want to get into it.

He looked away, out the window for a second and then went on.

"It's no big deal. Not compared to your story. I dated a woman for a long, long time. We were together through some pretty big events in my life, my dad's death, Drew's illness, you know, that stuff. Anyway, she was there through it all and I mistook that for love and dedication and I mistook my feelings for her for true acceptance of my Dad's death. Because of my misunderstanding about her and about what I really needed at that time in my life, I threw myself, my heart and everything at our relationship and, even when we were off and on, I never stopped loving her. That saying, though? Love is blind? It's true. In my case at least," He laughed a hard, brittle laugh full of self-loathing.

"What do you mean?" I asked.

"I mean that I let myself think that we were more than we were and that she was better than she was because I loved her. I loved her enough to propose and I was an idiot for doing it."

"That's not idiocy Jacob. That's sweet," I said matter of factly.

"I was an idiot because I was blind to what was going on right under my own nose. She had been cheating on me for years and I didn't even know it. With a friend of mine actually, the friend that I had asked to take pictures of our engagement, and she felt the need to inform me after I had made a fool of myself on one knee. Instead of saying yes to my proposal, she told me that she was already planning on eloping with the other guy. I was too late."

"Well, she sounds callous and egotistical and, well, just plain cruel! You're better off without her Jacob." I said with anger rising up inside of me.

"I am. You're right. But for the longest time, I didn't realize it. I'm still coming around to realizing it actually, along with a whole bunch of other things. Here's the point in my telling you this, though, Willa. I don't know what it's like to walk in your shoes exactly but I know how hard it is to find yourself and your life after the person you thought would be in it with you is gone.

I don't know how you feel, only you do. But don't you see? You know how you feel! You just told me how you feel so that tells me something."

I had started crying again from his story and mine. It was all just so much sadness and it enveloped me. He was calm, placid, unmoved, though except for his eyes. I could see the spark in them, the joy of hope.

"What?" I said in a huff as I wiped the tears from my face.

"It tells me that you know your heart and if you know your heart, then you know who you are."

Was he right? Did I know my own heart? I thought that it was too broken to be known, battered beyond recognition. I looked at him then for a long minute, trying to decide if I wanted to accept this diagnoses.

"My heart is a mess," I finally said.

"So is mine. So is everyone's."

"I don't know if I want to know myself without him."

There. I had said it. That's what it all boiled down to. I had always been a part of a whole; Willa and Ollie but that whole was severed. I was a half abandoned like a starfish that lost its limb. I knew that a starfish could regenerate what it had lost, that eventually, the thing that had only been a fraction of something was a whole again. Did I want to do the same?

Jacob leaned over across the table and grabbed both of my hands. I was taken off guard by how large and soft and warm they were. Not in a clammy kind of way, just warm like a heating blanket wrapped around my fingers.

He looked me in the eye and held my gaze for a moment. We grew quiet and it was easy and peaceful.

"Willa, I don't want this to come across as harsh so please understand that when I say this, I mean it in the gentlest and most encouraging way possible," He paused for a second and then went on. "Ollie will always be a part of your story, a part of your heart but here, physically, you are without him. You are here, alive, present and you are a whole person. I'm telling you this because I wish someone would have said these things to me when I was grieving after my Dad died. Maybe then, I wouldn't have searched for wholeness somewhere I shouldn't have. Maybe then, I wouldn't have lost myself for those years. I know you might not want to know yourself without Ollie. For awhile, I didn't want to know myself without my Dad, without Jenny, but that's all that there is now. I want to know you and I think you do too."

Then he smiled that closed lipped, half smile he has, like a fish hook was stuck in one corner of his mouth pulling him up and out of the water, up and out of this moment. He let go of my hands and placed them on the table. He pushed himself up, using the table as a point to push off of or maybe it was more like he was pressing all that had been said down into that space. He was leaving it there for me to fill up with. Like every word he had just said was a platter full of food for my heart and soul to dig into. He walked out of the Café, without saying another word and I watched him go matching his silence with mine.

Something had changed in that moment. A subtle shift in my existence. Not because the words he said were too harsh. I knew they were true. I knew that I was here and Ollie was there and we would never be us again. I knew that everything was different and I had spent the better part of two years trying to figure out what that meant and who I was. I had gone back and forth between searching desperately for this new identity and abandoning the search all together but now, well now Jacob had inserted himself into the quest. He had stated plain as day that he wanted to find this missing person as much as I did and for the first time since Ollie died, I felt like I had a partner.

There in that empty café, with the snow falling down outside, I finally felt like I wasn't alone.

* * *

A week later I sat at Lil's desk with a perfectly organized, beautifully sorted, spectacularly in order mess in front of me.

I had done the impossible; I had formulated a way to organize her balance sheets and expenses so that it actually made sense. I had done her taxes, both business and personal so that she would be getting a much larger return than ever before. I had even found a few areas that she could tighten up to increase her profits and thus increase her salary a bit but still, it wasn't going to be enough.

Not enough for Princeton, that is, which was where Drew was going.

He had received his acceptance letter two days prior and my heart leaped and sunk all at the same time.

He had stood there in the doorway to the café with a big, one-thousand-watt smile on his face. Just stood there silently but his face, coupled with the huge 8x10 size envelope in his hand with Princeton's logo on it spoke all the words anyone needed. Lil took one look at him and started jumping in the air and clapping, her red, curly hair flying around her like confetti shooting out of a popper.

"You did it didn't you?" she asked him with tears streaming down her face.

He just nodded, that big smile with his perfect Princeton teeth gleaming pulling on my heart strings. Lil ran to him and nearly knocked him down with a hug that resembled a tackle. The café erupted in applause because our boy, he was our boy, had gotten into Princeton of all places.

The kid who served us all with the sweetest smiles, who's laugh filled the place like Jacob's music, who's kindness walked the older customers to their car and shoveled the walks of the entire block, he had done it! I couldn't help but tear up at the beauty of it all, couldn't help but be swept up in his joy until I heard what he said to his mom, quietly, humbly, with resignation and conviction.

"It's cool to know that I did it Mom, but I'm not going. It's too expensive."

"Nonsense!" Lil said. "We'll find a way. Willa's helping me find a way."

And that's where my heart plunged to the floor.

I was trying to help her find a way but I couldn't invent one out of thin air.

I gave Drew a big squeeze and tearful congratulations as I passed by to hole up in the office and had barely left since then. I had to find that money somewhere for him. If any kid deserved to go to Princeton, it was Drew and I was bound and determined to make it happen.

So, there I was, trying to make money grow on trees through sheer diligence and triple checking what I had already done when Lil tapped on the door.

"From the looks of this place, things seem to be in better order than they've ever been. Does that mean that you've done it?"

"Done what?" I asked nervously. I knew what she meant but I was biding my time.

"Found my Princeton pot of gold! Found a way for me to make some more money so I can fill that boy's head with college learnin'," she said with a smile.

I sighed a long, heavy sigh and said, "Lil why don't you sit down." I tried to get up to offer her her chair but she waved me off.

"You know I never come in here and work. That chair is more yours than mine now," she said as she pulled a stool over from the corner. I hadn't even been aware of its presence the first week, so buried was it under papers.

"Alright. Say what you need to say," Lil said.

"Ok. I've looked at everything from every possible angle. There were certainly some areas that I found that you could make some changes and I laid them all out for you here," I said handing her a report I had made. "They're little changes, places that you could cut back costs, possible items on the menu that cause you to spend more than you make on them, slight room rate increases that are in line with the market nearby, things like that. I've also finished up your taxes and I don't mean to say this in a boastful way, but I think you'll find that they're the most thorough you've ever had. You should be getting a better return this year both personally and business wise than you have before."

"That's amazing, Willa! You're a wizard! I'll do all of this stuff, use that money from the government for Drew's tuition and we'll be right on track!"

"Well, it's not that easy Lil," I said handing her another packet of information. "I took the liberty of looking into tuition costs and financial aid information for Princeton as soon as we heard that Drew got in. I don't need to tell you that Princeton is about as good an education as he can get and they know it over there. It's expensive, Lil. Really expensive. More than this stuff is going to cover."

Lil sat quietly on the stool thumbing through all of the papers that I had given her and with each turn of a page, her perfect, poised, confident posture began to dissipate. She was slouching, the pose of dejection and I had never seen her like this before. Her eyebrows pulled together in concentration and her shoulders hunched over herself like she was carrying a burden that was too heavy. It was all I could do not to just snatch the things out of her hand and shred them up, to say, "Forget all of this! We'll find a way!"

"What am I going to do Willa?" She finally said quietly. "How could I have been so naïve to think that we could cover these costs?"

"Don't worry Lil! There are ways to pay for this! Student loans or work-study programs…" I began but she cut me off with conviction and fire in her voice.

"I don't want him paying for this for the rest of his life. I don't want to saddle him with that debt just because I couldn't find a way to pay. I don't want that for him! He deserves to start his life with nothing but ease and good things," She was starting to sound panicked and I could hear tears choking her.

"Ok Lil, ok. Don't worry! We'll think of something. Don't worry! Don't give up yet." I said as I crossed the few feet between us to give her a hug. It wasn't something I would have done three months ago for anyone, but this woman, this beautiful woman that I now called friend would have done it for me and I knew that's what she needed. She had changed me, softened me and the least I could do was to try and hold her together as she cracked.

She sniffed and wiped her eyes as we let go of each other and she looked me long and hard in the eye.

"Why do you care so much about this Willa?" She finally asked. It wasn't like her, to ask someone why they felt something. She usually knew already and told the person before they did. She knew hearts better than anything so I figured that she must need to hear it from my mouth, hear that I loved her and her son like family, hear that she didn't have to carry this alone. That she had a friend and someone to lean on.

"Lil, you know that I came here broken. I didn't think that there was goodness left for me in the world or that I would ever get to see happiness like Ollie and I had again. But then I met you and Drew and Jacob. I got to see your happiness and selfless, strong, love and interdependence on each other. I got to see the beauty that love can take in a different form, the bond of mother and son and, I swear on Ollie's grave, that it nourished my starving soul," I was tearing up at this point and so was she but it was too late to stop.

"It fed me Lil, because it gave me hope. And then, as if just being around all of you and your cosmic, beautiful bond wasn't enough, you let me in. You let me be your friend and join your world. You told me the things that I needed to hear and you spurred me on to live a little bit more. You made me dance again Lil and that's profound and amazing and all things good. Bottom line, you're my friend that's like my family. You've given me a home and something to smile about and that's why I care. I care about seeing you and Drew happy."

Lil smiled through her tears and enfolded me in another hug.

"Well then," she said, "I think we'll figure it out. With all of that behind us and pushing us on, we'll figure it out."

"We will," I said, "I promise."

And I had never meant a promise more. I had also never been so unsure of how I would keep one...

Chapter 14

Jacob

I sat across from her, letting the silence become comfortable. This was our fourth session and still, she had said nothing. She was sixteen and silent, sixteen and sad. She sat in front of me looking down at her hands letting her stringy brown hair fall in front of her face like a veil, like a mask, like a curtain hiding my view into her mind and heart.

She had grown up in foster care, shuffled from home to home like a pawn of the state until her parents had adopted her last year. They seemed like a great couple, older with kind faces and gentle demeanors. They were soft in every sense of the word and their new daughter, the one that they had spent years hoping for was hardened. Hardened by what I suspected was a childhood full of neglect, anger, abuse, I wasn't exactly sure but I hoped to find out.

I could see the hope in her mother's eyes at the end of every session. She would walk up to me while her daughter walked to the car and say, "Did she say anything this time?"

"Not yet." I would reply "but she will. We just have to wait."

So we did. We had been for a month now but I wasn't discouraged. I had seen this before and I knew what to do.

We sat in silence for the first five minutes, letting the quiet tuck itself in around us. Finally, I looked at her and spoke.

"Anya, how was school today?"

She looked up but not at me. She just stared out the window.

"Yeah, I never really liked that question either as a kid. I mean, it was school, it just was what it was am I right? Not exactly the first place you would choose to spend your day I'm sure."

She kept staring out the window.

"Where would you like to spend your time? If you could go anywhere you wanted, where would it be?"

Nothing. No response.

I decided to change tactics.

"Anya, I get it. I've picked up on your clues. You don't want to talk to me and that's completely fine. There are other ways to communicate, though, other ways to get whatever is going on inside of you out in the open. Do you like music?"

She jerked her head towards me quickly and I saw her eyes change from listlessness to excitement for half a second. She seemed to have some reservations about showing that though because before I knew it, they reverted back to their sad state and she simply nodded that yes, she did like it.

"Good," I said. "Me too. I've always thought that music captured my feelings better than words. Do you agree?"

She shrugged but I knew I might be on to something.

"Well, here's what I'm going to do. I'm going to get out my guitar and start playing some songs. All you have to do is sit there and listen. Just sit and listen and if I start playing a song that sounds like how you feel, just let me know ok?"

"Fine," she said. It was a pinprick of a sound but still, it was there, marking the room with her presence.

I grabbed my guitar and started playing. Upbeat songs at first with a steady, quick rhythm, the kind that happy people would tap their toes to. I knew this wouldn't draw her out but I wanted to start somewhere else so she wouldn't feel like this was a ploy. I wanted her to simply feel the music, happy music.

I wanted to deposit it into her soul like a good meal because I believe with all of my heart that that's what music does; it feeds our souls.

I strummed and played, songs that I knew by heart, letting the melodies run together, inviting her into the presence of it all. We stayed like that for a few minutes. I would look up at her every once in a while and she would look the same as the last time but slowly, as I let the tempo slow ever so slightly, she relaxed. I saw her shoulders lower and her hands unclench. I saw her ease into the couch and look around the room with interest.

I knew it was time.

I let my hands move into the proper fingering, let them get in position for feeling and sadness to flow through them. I began to play in a minor key, slow and steady ascending and descending chords in half steps. They were the tiny, ever-changing movements of sadness, like tiny little cuts to the heart. I strummed and played swaying to the song and looked up ever so slightly.

There she was this wounded bird of a girl on my couch, sitting with her eyes closed. She swayed gently with her hands clasped in her lap. I almost stopped playing because I wanted to cheer, to clap that she was engaging, she was feeling but I kept going. The music was unlocking her heart and there was more to tell.

I played that minor, slow song, letting the hurt and sadness that it echoed seep into her and out of her. I let it wash over her and pull out what was inside her soul; all of the sad stories and crushed hope, all of the disappointment and anguish, it leaked out with every note. Tears were falling down her cheeks now, steadily washing her.

The song was speaking for her.

I changed the tempo up, strumming faster, harder, rapidly moving my hands along the frets. It was still a minor chord progression but this part wasn't slow and keening. It was hard and mad and fast and strong, like a waterfall of anger pushing itself downward through the room.

I hoped my guess wasn't off, I hoped that I hadn't moved here too quickly, but I had a sense that she was equal parts sad and mad. I wanted to guide her to look at all of it, to feel it all, to validate it all, so I played. I strummed hard and fast and scowled with every stroke of my hands. I felt it and hoped she did too.

She did.

There she sat with her jaw clenched and her eyebrows pulled together tight over her closed eyes, like a needle of pain and a thread of anger was sewing them together. The tears were falling harder and her shoulders moved up and down as she began to sob silently. She clenched and unclenched her hands, adding a rhythm all her own to the song and I matched her pace.

I followed her hands and her shoulders and her sobs until she was the percussion section to my playing. Until the music was in her. Until she and I were playing the song of her heart.

The song built and swelled and still she cried. She put her head in her hands and bent forward on the couch. She was bowing, surrendering to her feelings, to her story and she was letting the music reveal it all, letting it take center stage and together we basked in its presence.

I saw her there in that place of feeling, that deep and anguished place of remembering and acknowledging, of wondering and hating and hurting and I knew it was time for the end. I knew that I would shift the song for the last time but I would guide it away from anger and hurt.

We would end with peace.

So I played a soft melody of gentle, major chords. No dissonance, no half steps. I played full, leaping thirds, and fifths; the movement of completion, of order, of happiness. I played with a gentle strum and a slow, pretty pace and I watched her find quiet. The sobs stopped, her breathing slowed. I saw her take a deep breath, filling herself with air that was humid and heavy with her song.

Her eyes were still closed but I knew she was seeing it all, all of who she was and what she carried inside of her. I knew that the songs had pulled it from her like weeds and she was realizing that there was still fertile soil inside her heart. That those weeds had been sucking her life away for too long, sucking out the goodness within her but that goodness was still there. Still hers for the taking.

I saw her fill herself up with the peace that the song offered. I saw her accept it and then I stopped playing, leaving her with silence once again.

We waited like that for a minute or two, letting the last note of the song fall to the ground. Like dust that had been disturbed, the air and light in the room were full of its particles and we simply waited for it all to settle in. I watched her as the tears stopped and her eyes opened, I watched as she opened really.

"You feel don't you?" I asked quietly.

"Yes," she said.

"That's where we'll leave it then, Anya. You did very, very well today. I'm proud of you."

Tears sprung to her eyes again and she smiled.

"Thank you, Dr. Hawkins."

"Thank you, Anya, for letting me in. We'll pick up again next week."

I walked her to the door and led her over to her mother. Her mom stood up when she saw us coming and took one look at Anya's tear stained face. She turned to me with a question in her eyes. I knew what she was asking and I simply smiled and nodded.

She broke out in a grin that took over her whole face, like a crescent moon in a picture frame.

We said our goodbyes and I watched them walk out the door. Anya walked next to her mother and hesitantly, hopefully, beautifully reached for her hand. They stayed like that until they got to the car and I saw them break apart with trust and hope and joy in their eyes and I knew, we had started something.

Joy surged through me as I turned away from the scene outside until I turned around and saw Willa, sitting in the corner. I had completely missed her presence in the room, focused as I was on Anya and her mother. Angie had left early for the day so we were alone in the waiting room. She sat there, though, in a chair across from my office door holding a cup of coffee in her hand and tears in her eyes. My heart caught at the sight of her.

"Willa, what are you doing here? Are you ok?" I asked.

"That song. What was it?" She asked.

"Oh, I don't know really. A mix of songs you may have heard and others that I made up. Why?"

"Because, well, I can't explain it really, but it felt like it knew me." She sniffed and wiped a tear from the corner of her eye in the way that women do, with their middle finger gently swiping so as not to disturb their make up. It was endearing.

"I mean, I walked in here while you were playing because Lil asked me to drop off some coffee for you on my way to an appointment and it was so weird! It was like a song had been written about me or for me or, I don't even know but whatever it was, it was so moving. I just sat here and cried and felt and wondered, you know?"

I went over to her and sat down in a chair next to her. The table in front of us was littered with magazines that teenagers would like.

"I do know. I get it I mean, the way that a song can do that to you. Did it feel good?"

"Yeah, it did. Your music made me feel sad and mad and peaceful and... *good* and I can't say that I've been able to say that in a long time. That's some super power you have there, Jacob," she said with a small laugh as she fished for a tissue in her purse.

"It's not a superpower it's just the way music and feelings work. It heals."

"Not everyone's music Jacob, only yours."

She stared at me for a minute after she said that. She stared hard with concentration and focus but with a tenderness that I hadn't seen in her before. It seemed like so much was going on behind her green eyes. They were like a flower stem emerging in spring, the tip, the culmination of all that was happening underneath the surface and I waited for whatever she was feeling, whatever she wanted to say to bloom. In the meantime, though, I was content to watch her, content to listen.

We were so close to each other, our thighs brushing. I could smell her hair again, just like I could on the sled and I wanted that smell to fill my lungs forever. My hands tingled as I held them in my lap, held them back from grabbing hers or worse even, from running them through those fragrant tresses. She had leaned into me ever so slightly but she was close enough that I could see the tear streaks on her cheeks. Close enough that I could have kissed her.

"Actually Jacob, I might regret saying this later but maybe I won't, and maybe it's just because I'm in a psychiatrist's office and there's some truth serum emitted through the ventilation system but whatever it is, I have to say it. It's not just your music that heals or makes people feel good. It's you. You do that because you care and listen and empathize. You are a good man Jacob and I'm grateful for you. I'm grateful that you make me feel..."

She trailed off then as if she was catching herself and my heart dropped like her sentence. My heart and her unsaid words tumbled together but I could imagine what they were. I could imagine it by the blush in her cheeks and the way that she suddenly looked down at her hands and the way that all of it made me hope for her to say that she simply felt for me. That I made her feel and long and hope for *me*.

"Oh! I almost forgot! Here's your coffee," she said as she shoved the cup into my hands spilling a little bit on my hand in the process. It wasn't very hot anymore but she still seemed concerned.

"Oh gosh! I'm so sorry! Do you have any tissues in here so I can wipe that off? I'll find some!" She whirled around looking for a box of tissues but her eyes landed on the wall clock instead.

"I'm late for my meeting with that lawyer!" she said with surprise and exasperation.

"What lawyer?"

"The lawyer, for the thing for Drew." She mumbled while she fished in her purse for her keys.

"For Drew? What do you mean? Is he ok?" I asked. The moment had turned so quickly and my mind couldn't keep up but concern was inching its way into the place that joy and anticipation had been.

"Huh? Oh yeah! He's fine! It's nothing to worry about. Just, umm, well I can't say yet ok? I've got to go Jacob! I'm so sorry! See you tonight at dinner? Bye!"

And just like that, she was gone. Before I could say anything, respond to her words or her look or, if I wasn't mistaken, the longing in her eyes, she was gone. I felt her absence, the aloneness of the room but the presence of what she had said and the way that we had connected was still there.

I wished she had stayed so that I could have said more and

heard more and felt more but that was fine, it would just give me some time to come up with something to say later, and say it I would.

* * *

A few hours later, I made my way to the café to give Drew his guitar lesson. Of course, with thoughts of Drew came thoughts of whatever it was that Willa was talking about earlier. Actually, those thoughts had dogged me since she left and worry had begun to creep in.

"What could he need a lawyer for?" I asked myself as I shifted my guitar from one hand to the other so I could lock my office door.

He wasn't a kid that got into trouble. Ever. And if he was in trouble, why would Willa be handling things and not Lil? Things just seemed off and I had to know what was going on. I loved Drew too much and was too proud of him to sit back and let things happen in his life without my involvement. That wasn't how things had happened ever before and it wasn't about to start now. Not with Princeton on the line. I decided I had to ask Drew and Lil about it as soon as I got to the Café. I couldn't let myself wonder any longer. It was enough to ask my mind not to worry about whatever was going on between Willa and I and the almost moment we had had again today. I couldn't worry about Drew too.

Ten minutes later, I was at the Aurora Boreal sitting up in Drew's room with him and Lil. The room had remained mostly unchanged since he was a little kid. It still was painted a metallic silver to make it look like the inside of the spaceship that it was on the outside. There were still glow in the dark stars hanging on the ceiling, the same stars that Drew had stuck up there while he sat on my shoulders, his bald head that chemotherapy had gifted him gleaming in their glow. Still a Denver Broncos poster hanging next to his window. The only marked difference, the only big difference, was the Princeton poster hanging on his closet door. That was Drew. Consistent, solid, passionate and unchangeable. And bound for greatness.

"What is it, Jake? I've got dinner to prepare for!" Lil asked. I had insisted that we have this discussion now and Lil was none too happy to have me barking orders at her.

"I want to know why Willa had an appointment with a lawyer for 'the thing for Drew' as she put it," I said rather emphatically with my arms crossed over my chest. I looked over at Drew and said, "I can't imagine that you are, but if you're in any kind of trouble at all Drew, you can come to me!"

"Trouble?" Lil said. "Drew has never been in any kind of trouble that constituted a lawyer in his life. And he never will be," she said the last part with her eyebrows raised and a finger pointed in Drew's direction.

"Well, then what's going on?" I asked as I threw my hands in the air. I was shocked that neither one of them seemed the least bit upset or even curious about this whole thing. In my mind, the word "lawyer" elicited a certain level of concern, intrigue, unease even but them? It was like any other day.

"Beats me," Drew said with a shrug. He had picked up his guitar and started tuning it while we talked. "Maybe she meant a different Drew."

"I don't think so," I said.

"Jake, don't worry. Willa loves Drew and she would never do anything but seek his best interests out. I'll just ask her when she gets back. It doesn't need to be some big problem that we have to have a secret family meeting about. I'll just ask her," She shrugged and looked at me, waiting to see how I would respond.

"I don't mean to imply anything negative about Willa here. I would never do that. Whatever she's doing, I know she's doing for Drew's good. I just need to know what it is."

"Then let's just ask her," Lil said again but this time, with a laugh.

"I want to be there when you do. I need to know what's going on, ok?" I was exasperated and it was showing. I was worried and it was showing.

Lil smiled at me and patted me on the cheek. "Ok, Uncle Jake. I wonder if you could love that boy any more than you do?"

"I don't think so but then he keeps doing things that make that love grow."

"Yeah, like this awesome guitar riff!" Drew said as he launched into a clumsy solo.

"Or, like getting into Princeton," I said as I leaned against the poster on his closet door. "*That* right there was not anything to brag about. Scoot over and let's start your lesson. And Lil, come get me when Willa get's here."

"So we can ask her about the lawyer thing," Lil said.

"That. And other things."

"Like what other things, Jake?" Lil said with raised eyebrows.

"Like what she's doing for dinner on Friday night," I said. I didn't say it breezily or in an off-handed way. I said it purposefully, intentionally, if only to convince myself that I actually would be asking her. That my mind was made up and even my own mind couldn't convince itself that this wouldn't happen.

"Finally!" Lil said as she threw her arms around me. She put both of her hands on my face, cupping it like a mother would a child's and smiled. "Finally," she said again softly and then, she turned and walked out the door with a loud "Wahoo!" punctuated by a fist pump for good measure.

I laughed and looked over at Drew waiting for his reaction. I expected him to at least shake his head at his mom but instead he pumped his arm and hollered in a perfect imitation of Lil.

"What?" he said. "I'm with her!"

Chapter 15

Willa

By the time I made it back to the Café, dinner was well on its way and the band had made it through three songs. I was later than I had expected but it had been a long and drawn out afternoon filled with, well, all kinds of things.

I felt like I had been pulled through a wringer. Those old things that people used to do their laundry with.

My Grandmother had one in her basement when I was a kid and Quinn and I used to go down and look at it in awe. Like it was some kind of magic thing, a time machine or a torture device or something that you were supposed to cook with maybe. My Grandmother found us down there just staring at it one day.

"It was my mother's." She had told us. "We used to do laundry with it every Friday when I was a little girl. She gave it to me in her will and I've been using it ever since."

She showed us how she used to pull the clothes through it when she was little, and I was captivated by the fact that if that machine could talk, it would tell us how it had seen those hands forever and always. It could probably tell us when each scar or age spot appeared or what they looked like in miniature. It could tell us that her hands were the same as her mother's and it would probably recognize mine and Quinn's as the same make and model. The same hands just different generations.

She would wring out all of the water drip by drip, careful not to get her fingers stuck in it but to do a complete and thorough job. We were mesmerized, Quinn and I, and we begged her to let us try. We spent many afternoons down there with her, wringing out our clothes and wringing out story after story from her.

It always fascinated me, the fact that she chose to use her old wringer. She had a perfectly good electric dryer not five feet away from it, tucked in the corner of her basement. She only used it as a surface to fold clothes on, though. I asked her why one day as we carefully fed one of her high-collared nightgowns through the wringer and her answer had played back to me all day long.

"Willa, that electric dryer would be faster for certain. It would take my clothes and spin them around in that heat and it would force the wet right out. But, honey, there's just something about this that does my soul good every so often. Something about tending to the things we wear, the things that cover our whole selves, hearts and all with slowness and steadfastness. It's just good."

I was still a little confused so I pressed her for more.

"What do you mean Grandma?" I asked, my voice floating over the sound of the water dripping into the basin below the wringer.

"I mean that it's good to remember that the stuff of life, the stuff that we wear over our hearts sometimes needs careful and vast and detailed attention. Sometimes, we have to make sure that we wash away all of the mess by hand and then watch it fall away drip by drip."

I still remember the look in her eyes as she said it. The intensity and gentleness finding a perfect balance like the treble and bass clef do in a song. Complete opposites joining up to carry it. That's what her eyes were like; a song. They moved and rose to a crescendo. They had dynamics and nuances and beauty and above all, they took you somewhere that nothing else could and my heart wanted to follow so badly.

"Come turn this wheel honey, will you?" She asked me. I walked over to where she was standing and began to crank the wheel of the wringer, my strength making the mechanism grind on.

"Look at your arms, Willa. Look at the muscles flex and grow. You're getting stronger with every turn."

"I guess so," I replied.

"You are, my dear. That's why. Letting yourself take the time to wring it all out, to watch the waters of cleansing fall away and see a pressed down but clean and ready garment come forth, that makes you strong Willa."

There was a fire in her eyes now, enough to dry the clothes all on their own.

"That's life, my girl. Sometimes, we have to let the wringer take the things that our hearts wear. It will take longer, yes, but it will make you stronger and you'll never forget the way the water fell away. You'll never forget the way it all came out dry and ready on the other side," She patted my face and gently moved me aside to finish the job for me but not before she kissed the top of my head, sealing her words in its depths.

I knew that it was poetry. That the drip drop of the water and the squeaking of the age old crank was the percussion section to her stanzas but never did I understand it more until this day. Until this season of making my way through the wringer ended.

Because, today, it had ended.

Not in a pronounced way, one where I could seal up all the heartache and memories and ship them off somewhere. It wasn't a tidy ending like in a movie or anything. It just was time to wrap it up. The grief, I mean. Let me back up.

I had sat in Lil's office for hours on end trying to come up with a way for her to pay for Drew's schooling but nothing would come. It felt like my thoughts were on an endless loop, a frustrating and desperate loop and I couldn't really pinpoint why I wanted it all so badly. I guess it was simply that I had fallen in love with this family the way that any person falls in love with their own family. I felt the same towards Lil as I did towards Quinn and that was an astounding and powerful and big truth for me.

This woman who had let me walk into her life and who had made a space for me to bring all of my hesitancy and grief and mess with me, actually, who had welcomed it all like a project or a challenge, she needed me now and I wanted so badly to come through for her. And not just for her but for Drew and yes, for Jacob.

For Jacob. So much of my thoughts and feelings were being claimed by him lately. By his big, gentle smile or his eyes, that bore depths into your soul, like a drill looking for diamonds. By his dark hair and his bright green eyes. By his velvety soft voice, and the way it made familiar songs sound new. By the warmth and vastness of his hands or the way I imagined his lips to feel and it was all so obvious to me that he was where I was going. That all of the sad stuff and mess of grief was finally leaving me and I knew where to go next.

I sat in Lil's desk chair, spinning it round and round with my toes, watching the light on the ceiling stay centered and bright while the rest of the room spun on its axis. I sat there thinking and the knowing of all of this; of the deep love I felt for these people, of the completion of my mourning, of my pleasure and euphoria that lay in my past but my hope for the same in my future, it all wrapped around me tight. Like with each turn of the chair, a ribbon was being coiled and, for the first time, it was a ribbon of joy. Of *joy*!

I stopped my spinning abruptly, as soon as I could name what I was feeling. I pictured that bright yellow ribbon of happiness and remembrance and love enfolding me in stripes and I knew. I knew what the bow on the top of the whole pretty package would be.

I ran upstairs, pulled open my top left drawer and grabbed the check; the one that had my first and last name typed next to a bunch of zeros, the one that had exactly eight tear stains on various portions of it, the one that I had been given in exchange for years of marriage and happiness with Ollie, the one that came in lieu of his life.

I grabbed it, and I left.

* * *

When everything was finished and it was all in perfect order, I felt completely elated and completely drained.

It was right. I knew it was all right. Like a puzzle or jeans that fit like a glove. There was not a doubt in my mind that all that I had set up and put into motion with that check was exactly what I had needed to do, what Ollie would have wanted me to do. But still, it was done and that meant that a lot of other things were done for me and I felt like I needed to mark the occasion somehow.

If I had been back in Austin, I would have gone to Ollie's grave. It seemed like a moment that called for that. I had just finally decided what to do with his life insurance money after all but honestly, I wasn't all that disappointed that I couldn't visit.

He had been way too full of life to visit him at a grave.

So I did something else instead. I went to the storage unit, my storage unit and I hauled out my wedding dress.

I opened the box, opened it up, and I fingered all of the delicate, flowery lace. I ran my hands over the train, the one that I had picked because it was just long enough to pool around my feet but short enough so Ollie wouldn't trip over it at our reception. I touched each and every bead along the neckline and pearl button down the back and I talked to Ollie. Like a crazy person.

"You would have loved this dress, Ollie. You would have looked me up and down from head to toe and whistled that long, low whistle you did on prom night. Quinn imitated that whistle when I tried this on for the first time because we both knew that you would love it. We knew this dress was the one because it reminded us of you and *you* had been the one."

I fell silent for a moment, simply remembering the way he used to look at me, the way he used to love me. They were good memories but thinking of them no longer hurt. They made me smile. I smiled and kept going.

"Well, Ollie, I did it. I cashed in your check. You probably think I'm crazy for waiting this long to do it but you always thought I was crazy so I couldn't let you down now could I?"

I sniffed and laughed at the same time, remembering the way he used to look at me when I rambled on or burst into laughter and tears at the same time. He would shake his head with wonder in his eyes and say, "You're just crazy you know it? Crazy enough to love."

"It's all going to do some great things for some great people and I think you would have been so excited about it. You would have lit up with that big Ollie smile and given high fives to anyone within arms reach of you. That was just who you were. Happy, all the time. Celebrating all the time. Finding something to smile about. All the time.

That's why you would have loved this. Because it's going to give people something to celebrate and smile about. It's given me something to smile about and that probably would have been your favorite part of all of it."

I started crying then because I knew that this was a goodbye. The one that I never said to him in Austin at his funeral or when I packed up his studio or his bedroom. I hadn't been ready then but I was ready now.

"I need to thank you, Ollie, for making your life all about making me smile. I noticed you know? I saw the way that you strove to put laughter between us as much as love, how it came easily to you but still you fought for that joy for us. I loved you for that and for so many other reasons, too many to name now but you know them. You know how I loved you. The thing is, though, I depended on you for that joy and when you were taken from me, it was too."

I sniffed again and wiped my eyes, determined not to let any tears fall on the lace.

"I've had a hard time finding joy for a long time now but I think finally, I've got some. It's not with you. I finally understand that it can't be, but still, I've found it again. You were my joy before and now I've found it for the now."

"Is it bad that I don't worry how you would feel about my moving on? Cause I don't. I don't worry about it because I know that you loved me more than yourself and you would want me to be happy. People do things like this, well, normal people don't go to storage units and talk to wedding dresses, but still, people go and talk to their loved ones at their graves and stuff because they want closure and permission to move on."

"That's not why I'm here. I think you've always been giving it to me. I knew from the day that that life insurance check arrived that that was what you were telling me. To move on, to live, to find joy somehow but I didn't want to. Despite your best efforts, I didn't want to let you leave me."

"Well, Ollie, my love, I came to tell you that today I finally did. I'm finally moving and living and maybe even loving again and well, I just wanted you to know."

"Thank you for letting me. Thank you for once again, helping me find joy and for once again, sharing it with others."

I hugged the dress to myself, one last time and then, gently put it back into the box. I didn't want to damage any of the beading or lace work so that it would sell easier. I had hung onto it long enough but now, I had said what I needed to say and had done what needed doing and it was time for the dress to follow suit.

It was dropped off at a second-hand wedding dress shop a few blocks up the road in less than an hour and I imagined I could hear Ollie, whistling that low, loud whistle of his while I did it.

Chapter 16

Jacob

She walked into the Cafe like the sun walks into the sky in the mornings. All brightness and lightness and power and warmth. Like she was ready to begin. Well, not just ready to begin but making the beginning herself, the signal, the leader, the first light of newness and I was ready to follow her.

She was as beautiful as ever, dark hair as straight and shiny and long as a waterfall at night, green eyes sparkling like spring, smile radiant. What was so captivating about her was her presence, though. Something had happened, something had changed within her and I could tell with a moment's glance. Of course, I didn't just give her a moment's glance, though.

No, I stopped and stared. I played some mindless chords on my guitar, hoping the band would follow my lead. "Instrumental bridge", I tried to tell them via mind waves. "Somebody solo or loop the chorus or something. Anything. Just let me stop and stare at the woman before me."

For a minute, it worked. We locked eyes, Willa and me, and it was as if power lines had been laid between us, carrying a current of electricity from her eyes to mine. I didn't know what had changed, what had come over her but something had and I was liking it. She smiled at me from the back of the room which was enough to make my heart skip a beat but what really stopped me in my tracks was her wink. She winked at me and I nearly fell off of my stool. Not because it didn't seem like her. Actually, the first thing that came to mind when I saw her eyelid flick and her thick, alluring lashes fan up and then down was her polka dotted shoes, the ones she had been wearing on the day that we put her stuff in storage.

Those, shoes, that smile, and that wink were the most real things about her. That's who she was and I knew, I knew beyond a shadow of a doubt that this woman, with her excessively big words and penchant for dramatics, with her heart that was broken and her dreams that were crushed, was made to laugh and be light in every sense of the word and I had to be the one to do it with her.

I ended the song and announced that we were taking a short break. Hopefully, I did all of that well. I still don't really know what I was doing in that moment. All I could think about was that wink and the way that it invited me to her. It wasn't seductive. It wasn't some "come hither" look. That wasn't Willa. It was, however, an invitation to come to her. It was as if she was saying "Come here, Jacob. Let's be happy together." Like we had a million jokes and things to laugh about and the rest of world could join in or not.

So, I went to her.

She was standing just inside the doorway to the café, the foyer behind her. It was a warm spring night and only the screen door was closed. Evening air floated in bringing the smell of fresh cut grass and daffodils. The sun was just beginning to set and I could see it paint the sky, it's final love letter to the day and all of it was the perfect backdrop for the beauty before me.

"So you're a person who winks now huh?" I said.

"I am. I wink and I smile and who knows what else I do," she said. She was buzzing with joy and I couldn't help but feel it and laugh.

"Well, can I ask why?" I said as I looked her in the eye.

"Jacob, have you ever gone swimming with your clothes on?"

"Umm, yeah, I think so."

"When I was a kid and I was taking swimming lessons, they made us come to class and swim in our jeans and t-shirts one day. It was to teach us how to tread water with clothes on, you know like if you ever fell off of a boat or someone pushed you in the pool or something. I know it's silly. Of course, you wouldn't need to tread water because you would have a life vest on if you were just on the deck of the boat and…"

"You would?" I interrupted laughing.

"Of course, you would! Why wouldn't you? Any sane person would wear a life vest on a boat…. And you're teasing me aren't you?" She smiled.

"Not teasing," I said with raised, sarcastic eyebrows. "Just admiring your thorough safety knowledge. I'm sure it surpasses everyone else's. Go on."

"Anyway," she said as she looked at me with a humor veiled by exasperation, "We had to learn to swim with our clothes on and it was the weirdest feeling. There's just so much resistance. The water can't move around your body like it's supposed to and you're so weighted down and heavy because all of it, every drop of the pool water is soaked up never to be surrendered by your jeans. It's the weirdest feeling. Like you're swimming but not really."

I was just listening now. I knew she was making a point and I liked how her mind worked, in metaphor and pictures.

"That's how I've felt for the past year and a half. Like I've been swimming with my clothes on. Just weighed down and heavy, like every drop of this whole mess I've been living has just clung to me and won't let me move on. I've convinced myself that I've been trying to get past it all. That's the getting in the water part. I'm in the swimming pool, living life, just not the right way. I'm not letting it all, all the stuff that life throws at me move around me and over me and make me learn to be weightless you know?"

"I do know, Willa," I said quietly, gruffly, because she was right. I knew she was right because I had been there, in the pool with jeans on and I had watched her do the same.

"Well," she said as she grabbed my hands and squeezed them tight, "Today I finally put on a swimming suit."

I laughed then because she said it with such joy and finality and I couldn't help but be happy with her. I pulled her into a hug then and held her close to me, breathing in the scent of her hair and the fit of her body against mine, trying with all of my might not to picture her in that swimming suit she was talking about.

"Well said, Willa. Welcome to summer," I finally said into her hair.

She pulled away ever so slightly, just enough so we could see each other. "Jacob…" she said. Her voice was quiet and deep and full of emotion and I began to lean in slowly and steadily, ready to kiss the words off of her lips. "There's so much I want to say to you. So much I need…"

"There you two are!" Lil's voice cut in like a knife in a horror film, stealing my hopes and dreams and breath. I wanted to growl at her but Willa let go of me right away and started clapping her hands with joy.

"Lil!" she said jumping up and down. "There's something I have to tell you right away! Where's Drew?"

Lil laughed at Willa's display of excitement. "I'm not saying I don't like this side of you but I would be lying if I didn't tell you that I was a little bit concerned. What in Heaven's name has got you so riled?"

"I'm sorry! I'm acting like a crazy person! Winking and clapping and jumping! You guys are probably going to have me committed soon. I promise, though, when I'm done talking to all three of you, we'll be jumping up and down together. Now where's Drew?"

"I'm right here and I brought you some coffee. I don't think you need it, though," he said.

"I'll take it! Thank you," she said with a smile. "Ok, I'm just going to jump right in here," She took a deep breath and a sip of coffee and went on. "You're just the best Drew! Just the best kid I've ever met. You've overcome so much and you're so smart and you love your mom better than any son I've ever known and you're just so talented and hardworking and you and your mom have taken me in as a part of the family when I needed to be loved but, let's be honest, wasn't that lovable…"

She was waving her arms around to punctuate every nice thing she said and had started to tear up now. Maybe because the joy at the beginning of this conversation must have needed balancing out.

"Why don't I take that from you, Willa," I said as I grabbed the coffee from her hand before it spilled all over us. I put my hand on the small of her back and gently said, "No one could argue those things about Drew. You're absolutely right. Why does it have you so worked up, though?"

"Well, because he's so deserving and I get to be the one to do something about it. I'm not saying this as well as I wanted. This kind of thing deserves a ceremony or a plaque or something because I see this as a reward. For your diligence and dreams Drew, but also for the fact that you and your family have gotten me out this season of grief. I don't know anyone else who I would want to give this to."

She pulled a crisp, white envelope out of her purse and handed it to Drew and Lil.

"I went to the bank today and set up a trust fund for Drew. That was what my meeting with the Lawyer was about, Jacob. In it, is enough money to pay for Princeton for the next four years. I used a portion of Ollie's life insurance money for it and the rest of that money is going towards setting up a scholarship for kids like you, Drew. I'm calling it the "Oliver Drew Scholarship" after the man in who's memory it's made and the one who's efforts inspired it." She went over and put her arms around Lil and Drew who were completely dumbfounded and speechless. "You have helped give me purpose and joy again. You've given me a place to belong and people to call my own in this new life that I'm living. This is the least I can do." She pulled them into a hug and when they all let go, tears were flowing down each cheek.

"We..." Lil said.

"Don't you dare say you can't accept it!" Willa cut in. "It's mine to give and I give it to you."

"What I was going to say was, we are going to need some champagne," Lil said with a laugh and a loud "Wahoo!" She ran off to the kitchen to get the glasses and the whole walk from the doorway to the kitchen was punctuated with her telling every customer she could find that "Drew's going to Princeton!"

Drew was standing in the same spot holding the envelope between both hands like he was afraid to drop it. Tears were flowing down his cheeks and he couldn't stop staring down at the blank white surface.

"Willa, I know what Ollie meant to you and how much you loved him. For you to give me this... I just, I don't, I can't..." Drew said.

Willa walked over to him and lifted up his chin between her thumb and pointer finger. "I know. I know how much you appreciate it and that you don't know what to say and that you can't thank me enough. I know. That's why I gave it to you. Send me a Princeton T-shirt and we'll call it even ok?"

He laughed and sniffed through his tears and said "Ok" and then he picked her up into a bear hug and spun her and their laughter around.

When he put her down, she was flushed and radiant. She looked directly at me, with laughter in her eyes but her smile fell when she saw my face.

"You're crying," she said. She walked over to me and put her hand on my cheek, wiping a tear with her thumb. It was so soft and so small, like a flower petal.

"Beauty moves people, Willa and that was a beautiful thing you just did," I said, but it wasn't enough. "Actually, it wasn't what you did that was beautiful. It is who you are. Willa, you're beautiful. Absolutely, positively beautiful." I reached up and touched her face right back, letting my hand trail over her brow and then down her cheek. I let it fall away then but she grabbed it with her own and we stood there, in the doorway of the café like that.

"I've known it from the first time I saw you but I've fought it because neither of us was ready but today, now, we're ready so I'm just going to tell you what you are and how I feel and how I need you. There's so much to you, you're so complex and deep and every facet that I see captivates me. The way your mind works and your heart feels so deeply and the way you love, it's all beautiful. I could go on for hours but all of it would boil down to the same thing. I'm falling in love with you and I have to tell you. I need you to know."

We stood silently with our eyes locked for a split second letting my words sink in between us, watering the garden that would grow there. Then, she let go of my hand and slipped her arms around my neck.

"I'm so glad to hear that, Jacob," she said. "Because I've fallen in love with you too and what a pity it would be to love someone all by yourself." She drew up on her tippy toes until her lips were even with mine. She smiled as we shared the same breath, the same anticipation and then she quietly said; "Well, are you going to kiss me?"

"Yes," I said deeply. "I'm going to kiss you."

I pulled her closer and our lips met like magnets. Her kiss was soft and sweet but sure and strong and all of it, every second of it was perfection. We were lost there in that doorway, with spring air surrounding us and love growing between us until it all was punctuated by Lil, spraying us with champagne.

"This is the night where all of my dreams come true!" Lil said as she cheered and sprayed the champagne.

My band had begun playing without me but the music didn't sound thin, it was full, all of it, everything about this moment was full. The whole café full of customers was behind Lil and all of them cheered and clapped and hollered for us.

I didn't blame them one bit. This was right, what Willa and I had. We had found the place that we were meant to be and the person that was to stand beside us and there, christened with champagne and laughter, our love story began.

Epilogue

Willa

I asked Lil once why she named the café "The Aurora Boreal Inn and Café."

Drew was home for summer break, having finished two semesters on the Dean's List and he sat happily on a lawn chair holding Sophie's hand. We were all spending a perfectly perfect night in the backyard of the Inn, sitting under the pergola that had clematis climbing up and lights shining down. The summer air was sweet and warm, and it held the weight of memories and all things good the way that summer does. It seemed like the perfect time to reflect.

I assumed the reason was part pun, part space related for Drew's sake and that it didn't go much deeper than that. Still, I asked because the place had become so dear to me, so a part of me that I needed to know everything there was to know about it.

Of course, like anything with Lil, there was so much more to it than I had expected.

"Google it. Google 'The Aurora Borealis,'" she had answered, so I did.

So that night, with Jacob sitting next to me on the bed, and a thank you note from that year's scholarship recipient on the night stand, I looked up all that I could find. Page after page filled my laptop's screen and I threw myself at it. Norse legends and scientific studies, pictures taken by freezing tourists and hardy residents of the northernmost parts of the globe, all of it captivated me.

I stared at the beauty of it all. The way the dark, frozen, night sky moved and dripped and danced with colors, it was like women in gowns in shades of red and green and blue and yellow dancing on a ballroom floor. I let myself get lost in the screen for just a moment and Jacob looked on in amazement with me.

And then I started to read about the causes, the why behind this phenomenon that's as old as the world itself.

It's all about the earth's relationship with the sun. Well, really it's more than that; it's all about our relationship with the particles that the sun hurls at us. You see, the sun experiences violent storms all along its surface from time time. When this happens, the particles from these storms go flying towards the earth. The earth surrounded as it is by its magnetic field, can't help but pull those particles, those fragments of burning hot storm into its atmosphere and the collision, the meeting of the storm with the everyday, familiar molecules in our atmosphere causes something astounding to happen.

When those particles from the sun collide with our molecules, the atoms within the molecules are sent reeling. They are excitable, you see, they are susceptible to being thrown into a rapid fire, can't stop, I'll throw up I'm so dizzy spinning and they stay like that for a bit. Eventually, though, the excitement slows and the molecules begin to calm down.

After they have reeled and been electrified, set to buzzing and burning by the sun's storm particles, they calm down and that's when the lights come on. It's in the calm after the collision, the quiet after the storm that the night sky glows and brightens.

As the molecules that have been hit by the storm calm back down, as they find their new normal, they emit a light that's so brilliant and unexpected that it captivates all the world. From the first generation to see them, to the one looking at them now, those lights have shone and moved and electrified the night sky and they have never ceased to captivate.

I thought about Lil, the version of her that I hadn't known, the one that was the mother of a young boy, sick with cancer. The woman who was raising that little boy alone save for the help of her brother, who had every reason to feel sorry for herself and to run scared from life. I pictured her taking care of Drew, combing his hair as it fell out in clumps, tucking him into bed in the hospital, standing watch over his bed day in and day out without the support of the perfect, sick boy's father. And then I pictured her opening the Inn, I pictured her painting the sign that would hang over the door.

I saw her writing those beautiful, flourishing, bold letters with paint that was permanent and poignant. I could see the determination on her face as she named this place of new beginning and I knew why.

She had been sent spinning by the storms of life, of her galaxy, she had been hit hard and worry and fear and anxiety had excited her soul in all the wrong ways. But there, in that moment, as she painted that sign, she was calming down. She was relaxing into newness.

She was shining her brilliant light, colored and caused by the storm, but shining it all the same.

I knew what that was like.

I looked down at Jacob's hand, my husband's hand over my

rounded middle. I kissed him as I put mine on top of his and together we felt our baby move, felt her reach up towards the world.

We had been hit too. Storms had collided with our familiar lives at one point and we had done the spinning of anguish and loneliness. We had experienced it, done it, followed the course that life had set us on. It was part of our story, but now?

Now, we had settled into life with each other. We had found one another at the place that our stories had met and here we were, calming down, settling into life together.

There we were, finding joy and lighting up the night sky.

the end

Acknowledgements

Writing is a solitary endeavor. At some point, characters, and settings and stories reveal themselves to you and you feel a deep sense of joy and excitement at the opportunity to put it all on a page. And that's where everything lives for a while; in your head and on your page. It's a world all its own and only you and the people you've imagined live there.

It's a solitary endeavor until suddenly, it's not. There comes a point where you need other people to enter your world. You need their feedback, experience, knowledge, and encouragement or the stories and people that you've imagined and come to love will be no more.

This is where I get to say "Thank You" from the bottom of my heart to the people in my life who stepped in when my writing needed to move from an individual thing to a group thing.

First, I have to thank Jesus. I've loved him since I was a little girl and it's His love, provision, and guidance that inspired this story and the themes therein. He is the one who turns mourning into joy. He is the one who makes all things new. He is the one who guides us to a place where we can find healing and rest and it's for His purposes that we are made whole again. I hope that His heart is evident in these pages and that if you are searching for spring after a long winter in your life that you turn to Him.

Thank you to my husband, Scott. For years, he's listened to this dream and fanned it into flame. He's let me babble on about the stories that I had planned and never finished, he's proofread word after word, and offered unending encouragement and advice. He's pushed me to guard the time that I've carved out to write and has validated it in every way possible. He is the reason that I began this story and he is the reason that I finished it. Thank you, my love, thank you!

I also need to thank my parents. For gushing over the fictional Abigail Adams diary I wrote in eighth grade, for saving every one of my high school newspaper articles, for the "Blog Wednesday" phone calls, and for the countless words of encouragement you offered as I grew into becoming a writer, thank you! All of those things, along with your love, sacrifice, prayers, and advice shaped me and made me. I hope that you saw yourselves in all of the good parenting moments in this story. You inspired them. I wish I could express how grateful I am for it all! I love you both so much! Thank you!

Thank you to my Beta Readers! Thank you, Melissa, Alex, Lindsay, and Megan for weeding through typos and errors and finding a story worth finishing. Thank you for every text, email, comment, or note that you sent. I wish I could tell you how much I appreciated it and needed it but I can't. So, I'll just tell you that without it all, I never would have had the confidence and assurance that I needed to publish this story. Thanks for helping to get it across the finish line.

Thank you, Cassie, the CPA extraordinaire, who answered my questions about accounting with thoroughness and passion. Any errors that I have made in describing Willa's work and tasks are my own and are no reflection of Cassie. Thank you for sharing your knowledge and expertise!

Thank you so much to my family and friends for all of your encouragement and interest in my writing. On the days when things aren't flowing well and I doubt my ability, your voices fill my head and spur me on.

Thank you to my teachers for showing me how to read like a writer and for exposing me to writers worth reading.

Thank you to my kids for being who you are. Your existence and love has inspired me, motivated me, and molded my heart in countless ways and I can't imagine my world without you all in it. You are my dreams come true and I love you with all of my heart.

Thank you to Christa Holland for the beautiful cover and to Stacey Blake for the interior formatting. Without your expertise, this would not have been possible.

And thank you to you, my readers. Thank you for spending your time reading my words. I hope that you found it to be a worthwhile investment.

Thank you to all of you! I hope I made you proud!

About The Author

Kelsey is a wife and mother of three who lives in her home state of Colorado. She holds a Bachelors Degree in History from the University of Colorado Denver but it's collecting dust somewhere behind her kid's baby books. Now, she spends her time raising her little ones and writing during their nap time. You can find her writing about her faith, marriage, and motherhood on her personal blog, whilewemother.com or visit her author website, kelseylasherauthor.com.

Made in the USA
San Bernardino, CA
27 November 2016